My Brother's
WIFE

NICOLE HOUSTON

This is a work of fiction. While reference might be made to actual historical events or existing locations, the names, characters, businesses, places, and incidents are either the product of the author's imagination or are used fictitiously, and any resemblance to actual persons, living or dead, business establishments, events, or locales is entirely coincidental.

All rights reserved.

No part of this book may be reproduced or transmitted in any form or by any electronic or mechanical means, including information storage and retrieval systems, without written permission from the author.

Copyright © 2020 by Nicole Houston

Published by *Urban Rose Publishing*
Cover Design by *Aleksandar Novovic*
Editor: *Emily Fuggetta*

Join Nicole Houston's Newletter

Follow Nicole Houston

http://urbanrosepublishing.com

This book is intended for adults only. The sexual activities and scenarios represented in this book are intended for adult target audience only

OTHER BOOKS BY NICOLE HOUSTON!

ABOUT THE BOOK

Not everyone gets a second chance at love.

Newly free of her cheating ex-husband, thirty-three-year-old Linnet is a ghost of her former self—lonely, broke, and caring for their daughter on her own.

With the bills from her daughter's life-saving surgery staring her down, Linnet needs a lot of cash—fast.

A friend refers her to a gentleman's club. With reservations—but no other options—she joins the club, and with it, an unexpected face is back in her life: Bryan, her ex's brother. Gorgeous, handsome, and rich, every woman wants him. And somehow, he wants Linnet.

The stubborn, dominant man is still her ex's brother, though. Seduced by his mastery, she longs to surrender and submit to him. Letting her guard down and sharing both her body and her heart, though—that's going to take a lot.

Can Bryan bring back Linnet's smile—and help save her daughter's life?

CONTENTS

About This Book
Prologue
Chapter 1
Chapter 2
Chapter 3
Chapter 4
Chapter 5
Chapter 6
Chapter 7
Chapter 8
Chapter 9
Chapter 10
Chapter 11
Chapter 12
Chapter 13
Chapter 14
Chapter 15
Chapter 16
Chapter 17
Chapter 18
Chapter 19
Chapter 20
Chapter 21
Chapter 22
Chapter 23
Chapter 24
Chapter 25
Epilogue

PROLOGUE

THREE YEARS AGO

"What do you mean, you saw Mike with his secretary? What's wrong with that? They work together, after all," asks Nina, my bewildered best friend.

"I found her on her knees in front of my husband in our study. God, you should have seen their faces."

"And what was she doing on her knees? Did you see her doing anything wrong?"

"Damn it, Nina, whose side are you on? I know what I saw when I walked in on them."

"The side of truth. I've seen many marriages destroyed due to presumptions. So, what was the secretary doing on her knees? Don't tell me she was sucking your husband off!"

I knew where Nina was coming from. Her husband's misunderstanding of a situation involving her ages ago had led to their separation, but they're working on their marriage. After dancing around each other for the last few months, I'm glad they're finally reconnecting.

I want to believe Mike is innocent more than anything, but I know what I saw: Cynthia on her knees, between his legs.

It wasn't clear, since his desk covered her, but I didn't wait to see what she was doing. The humiliation I felt was a bitter pill to swallow. Mike has never trusted me to suck him off, no matter how much I asked—and then I find him with her between his legs?

When I met Mike, it was love at first sight. I've always trusted him completely. But who knows how long they've been sneaking around behind my back? The thought tears me up. I mean, when I met Mike for the first time, it was in Cynthia's company. I remember he introduced her as the glue that held their office together. I didn't think anything about it, but now I am questioning everything I thought I knew.

I've had this weird feeling every time I saw them together, but I always brushed it aside, convinced myself it was my insecurities playing up. Growing up, no one wanted me, and my stepmother said I had cringing issues.

All I ever wanted was a place where I could be welcome. My mom died when I was ten; Dad remarried shortly after. He never had time for me; they later had three kids, and I became the outsider at home, the afterthought. Everything was a struggle, and I couldn't wait to turn eighteen to leave.

I scraped, worked after classes, and managed to get a scholarship to college. I still have two more years until graduating with my nursing diploma.

Mike was my everything, my anchor and rock—and without him in my life, I don't know what I'll do.

Nina decided to take me out so that I can unwind, but I can't even enjoy a beer. I'm five weeks along, so beer is out.

I try to relax, to stay in the moment with my friend, but my mind is racing with anxiety. Tomorrow, I have to figure out what to do; I can't go back home to Mike. Staying at Nina's home is temporary, since she and Richard are reconciling. I can stay in a hostel until I'm well along, save, and find a tiny place where I can have my baby and hopefully raise it.

"Are you okay?" Nina asks me.

"I'm fine, just thinking," I tell her.

"Everything will work out in the end. Don't stress. It won't do you or the little one any good."

"Let me buy you a drink," I tell her, knowing she'll decline as usual. She comes from a well-to-do family, and she never lets me buy her a drink if she has her way—which she gets most of the time.

"Just hold on tight. I'll get you some orange juice from the bar."

I watch her as she heads there, and I can't help but see the eyes of all the guys locked on her ass. She's so oblivious to her beauty, but she has inner grace. Wherever we go, she always draws guys' attention, while nobody seems to notice me.

We've been friends for the last three years, immediately hitting it off when we met in our dorm on the first day of college. We've been inseparable since then.

I lean back in my chair, doing what I love doing whenever I'm in a bar—people-watching, imagining the kind of lives they lead. I watch discreetly, not wanting to draw attention to myself.

I avoid eye contact with the guys; I don't want some random guy to think I'm interested.

"Did you put a drop of scotch in my drink?"

"Just a drop. It won't hurt the baby. She knows Mom is stressed. Plus, I'll ask my goddaughter to sleep while Mom imbibes," she tells me as she takes her seat.

I don't argue with her about my baby; she's convinced I'll have a girl. When she gets these convictions of hers, I've come to realize she's rarely wrong.

Chapter ONE

LINNET
ONE YEAR AGO

"We ran the test, and the results are back. I'm sorry, Linnet, but she needs specialized care. Her condition isn't improving," the elderly doctor tells me.

She's been taking care of my daughter, who's always in and out of hospitals. I thought I'd reached the end, but it seems life is throwing me another curveball.

I dropped out of nursing school and moved to this tiny town when I could no longer pay rent. Life is quiet here, and the landlady gave me the option of taking care of her rentals in exchange for rent. She's a godsend, and I thank my lucky stars I met her when I did.

But Chayla—my everything—started having health issues once she turned a year old. She's been treated for asthma, pneumonia, and bronchitis. Last month, we had some visiting doctors doing check-ups on kids for free, so I took her in. And it's worse than I imagined. Her heart has a tiny hole in her right ventricle—which requires immediate surgery.

And all I can think about is how I can possibly come up with the money.

I leave the clinic in a daze. At least I finally understand what's been ailing my little girl.

I call Nina and update her on my girl's condition. I need someone to listen to me and a shoulder to cry on. She's out of the country, but I know she'll catch the next flight here. She's been helping refugees with her husband in Africa. Right now, they're somewhere in Rwanda.

I walk home, unaware of anything around me. By the time I reach the end of the street, I'm crying, the tears blurring my vision. The only saving grace is I that know my way home—I could walk these streets blindfolded.

Overwhelmed, I can feel my lunch making its way back up, I bend and throw up all over the pavement. The retching is so intense that I'm soon on my knees, heaving. I stay this way, since I'm too weak to stand up yet, until someone offers me their handkerchief.

I am grateful, and when I turn to offer my gratitude, I'm met with a brilliant smile from Nancy, the local kindergarten teacher. We're not close but always civil with each other in passing.

She offers me her hand and helps me to my feet.

"I won't ask what's wrong, but let me take you to that café over there, and you can get some water," she tells me.

Once we're seated, she asks for some warm water and hot chocolate. I take the water and immediately feel better. Soon, I'm telling her what had happened at the clinic.

"I can help, but how desperate are you?" she asks me.

I'm surprised by the question, and I let her know it. She asks me to be open-minded and listen. She tells me she has a way that I can earn the kind of money I need within one week.

I'm skeptical—$100,000 within a week?

She tells me of a club that will offer that kind of money—but it's top secret.

We part, and I promise to think about it, and she tells me that I have three days to do so before the club closes its doors until further notice. She refuses to answer my questions and tells me I'll get my answers once I sign up with the club.

After a lot of persuasion on my part, she reveals that it's a gentlemen's club, and they usually pay thousands a week.

I promise her I'll think about it and get back to her.

My sick daughter is just so weak. She's almost three, but you could mistake her for a year-old baby. Today, she's having issues with breathing, and I have to tilt her upside down to help her blood circulate properly. Even her nebulizer isn't helping.

I have started experiencing some sharp chest pains, and I'm sure my stressful life causes them. As I watch my girl sleeping fitfully, I make my mind up. But can I really go through with this madness?

I haven't had sex in almost three years, and I'm not stupid—I know a gentlemen's club entails sex with perverts. I consider all that could go wrong. I know fate hates me. That bitch and I have never been on the best terms, but for my girl's sake, I hope she'll be busy and let me be.

I email Nina and ask her to hurry; she's the only person to whom I'd entrust my angel's safety.

Though it's past midnight, I call Nancy—before I can talk myself out of it.

chapter TWO

BRYAN

I can't believe I'm doing this, but I love it too much to leave.

I have always been an ass—an arrogant one at that. After having endless women call you something, it becomes your truth.

I have always been bright, gotten excellent grades, went to college, and killed myself in the field. My passion for biology and my dad's desire for me to be a doctor pushed me to become the best surgeon in the region.

The pay is good, but I inherited my wealth from my ambitious and doting aunt on my mother's side. She had a small real estate company that was strategically situated during a local city expansion project.

I got the contract, and now I'm making millions practically in absentia. I'm good with people, though, which has helped the company's growth—that and its competent management team.

So when my best friend Joe invited me to join his club, I was skeptical at first. I mean, why I should pay a membership fee of fifty grand a year just to have sex, when I could have any woman

I want for nothing more than a gift or two?

Yes, I always get the ladies a parting gift. I don't keep anyone around for more than a week, lest they start planning our wedding.

But this club has opened my mind so much; I can't imagine how I got by without it. I knew I liked being in control in any relationship, but I didn't think there were others out there like me.

I'm a trained Dom, and I love it. But what I need now is what other Doms have—a good sub—only I haven't found one that pulls me towards her, someone who exerts that magnetic compulsion and makes me want to overpower her, conquer her completely and sate her wildest desires… In truth, such a woman would make me her slave. What I want, what I need out of love, is to have a woman who can reciprocate all of my desires and fulfill my longings. Someone who challenges me. I would marry a woman like that—if she even exists, which seems unlikely. But I'm more likely to find her here than elsewhere, so why not? I'm sure it's a fantasy, though, and most of the women I've met are worth a respectful and pleasant fling—but not suitable for walking alongside me forevermore.

Joe thinks expecting to find my missus in this crowd makes me old-fashioned or even deluded. He always says we should enjoy it while it lasts, then get a mouse to take home to Mama. For the most part, that's just what I do.

The club organizes competitions once every three months to introduce new (and unsuspecting) ladies to the lifestyle. I'm sure I sound cynical, but that's the truth.

But it's the club's way of giving back to society, and I have seen it work. We get fresh meat, and either they discover a new passion or they walk away enriched—often both. Nobody loses. Of the new submissives, ten ladies participate in an auction and get to spend one week at the club. They cater to the members' desires, and at the end of the week, they go home with their prize money.

This time, I'm among the lucky bastards who will participate in the auction. All I want is a woman who can follow simple instructions and has an insatiable sex drive. I want to have all my fantasies come true, but I know at the end of the week, we'll go our separate ways. Someone I can train to be what I want in the bedroom, who will gleefully take to my commands? It seems like too much to hope for, so I'll just stick to these carefully curated hookups until a miracle happens.

Two more days to go; we've done all the necessary tests, and I have been declared healthy. The club always enforces condom use, but it's good to know even the ladies have gone through testing; it eases my mind.

Today, we are all meeting to hear what the club chair has to say. They have agreed to bring several women before us guys, and there will be no competition.

All we have to do is interact with the ladies via a chat site and pick the one we feel we are most compatible with…it's a win-win situation, where the club gets to see firsthand how the ideal candidate behaves in real life. It's a good way to screen out people who act overtly crazy.

We all get registered into the chat app and issued pseudonyms. The club assures us that the ladies have signed a non-disclosure agreement, and everything is as it should be.

We will meet all the ladies online first, chat, and get to know them for a week, then meet them later, and spend another week in their company.

I don't know how I feel; I'm not too fond of chit-chat. I am sure I'll get the most boring lady in the bunch. So I decided to check into the chatroom later, hoping to catch someone still up.

Me: Hi, anybody home?

Angel: Hi. Yeah, I'm around, if that's what you mean.

Me: yes it is.

Angel: Let's get to know each other, handsome.

Me: What do you do for a living?

Angel: Charitable work. I'm on a few boards around town.

Angel: How about yourself?

Me: I'm in business and healthcare.

Angel: that's cool. I'd love to talk more about that. Which areas?

Me: it's been a pleasure. See you soon.

God, I'm pathetic; I can't even chat with a woman for two minutes without running out of material. I don't understand why my social suavity doesn't translate to these situations, but it's like the words get caught in my throat—or in this case my fingers. I always forget how to speak to people, asking the most inane questions, even though I long for dark, intense, intimate conversations. I want to reach into a woman's soul and challenge her with new sensations and thoughts and have her challenge me just as much.

It's a fantasy. A deep, quietly cherished one, but a fantasy, nonetheless.

And since I'm never going to have that, it's no wonder I love life at the club. I find a girl I'm interested in, and if she's interested, we don't have to talk much—apart from laying down the rules.

Linnet

I can't believe I'm doing this: having conversations with perfect strangers that I might end up sleeping with—or worse. This club is bizarre, and it's challenging my patience. I didn't think there'd be so much dull paperwork before getting to the interesting stuff, but I guess they have tight security. I almost wish I'd just tried stripping. But I need the money for my sweet baby, and besides, some part of me is longing for an adventure. It's so uncomfortable and strange, but it's only a week or two, I tell myself.

If I didn't need this money desperately, I would give them the finger. God, how many hoops does someone have to jump through just to get laid?

I mean, I'm doing this for the money, but what about these guys? Do they go through this every time they want to sleep with someone? I hope I get someone with whom I can at least enjoy sex.

I reconsider all the questions I answered in their questionnaire after the medical checkups. I had to make up some fantasies. Will these guys know I haven't had sex in three years? What would I even fantasize about? I miss it, but I've been working so hard that I haven't had any time for myself, let alone for self-love.

I remember all the books I used to read with Nina—she loves erotica, and I read them once in a while when I got bored. Sometimes we'd read things out loud and laugh at them. She had some pretty outrageous stories, and I can't lie; I used to enjoy those. But now it seems I'm the one who's going to wind up with some crazy anecdotes.

And now that Nina is here, I won't get a break. She wants every detail, and she won't take no for an answer.

"Just give me the highlights of what you wrote. You won't be breaking a contract. After all, it's your part of the deal...I'm not asking about these rich guys."

"I just wrote what I like and dislike in a guy. My limits, things that I won't do under any circumstances—and don't ask me what those are."

I tell her that I filled in all the blanks and hope for the best. I've been chatting with these guys, as well, but I don't tell her that because knowing her, she'd want to see the chats.

Some guys are just annoying, for lack of a better word; one is sure that he'll introduce me to ménages, and I'll enjoy them. I have a sex toy or two, but ménages? There is no way in hell I'll get into something like that in a week.

Another guy tries to convince me that I'll love pain; I mean, he was asking which I'd prefer most, choosing between a paddle, belt, or whip. No way will I let someone cane or whip me. How can I experience pleasure through pain?

Some part of me is excited and also equally nervous about the next week. If all goes well, I will have money for my girl and maybe get a decent workout.

But I'm not holding out for more than that.

In two days, I'll meet these men, and I'm nervous. Friday morning, Nina takes me to the spa by force, intent on helping me do this right. I get pampered, and I'm happy about it. Since I got waxed earlier on, I won't be overly sensitive down there tonight. The last thing you want is a rash greeting someone as he puts his face between your thighs.

I put on my signature purple lipstick; it goes well with my dark skin. Being black and curvy always made me self-conscious, but I have come to accept that my figure is natural and a gift, and therefore, I should own it.

I choose a short black dress and pair it with my favorite white boots, trying to feel physical confidence. Nina makes me feel good about myself. She says that I have a body made for sin.

I'm usually reserved. But, well, if I have to play this part, maybe I can enjoy it. My husband was the first to share my bed, and he never complained about my figure, that was for sure. His interest in me boosted my self-confidence. But his cheating nearly destroyed that. I've had to focus on my achievements and goals to feel good about myself, which isn't such a bad thing. But now, just focusing on my looks—it's weird. Part of me thinks no man could possibly want me… But in some way, I like it. Maybe.

 I'll go into the club with an open mind. I'm in this to get paid at the end of the week, but getting a man at the same time would be a bonus. Not a bonus I'm expecting, mind you. But then again, nothing in my life has gone the way I expected it to.

chapter THREE

I take a cab to the club, which has an innocuous appearance. It looks like a warehouse, but looks can be deceiving.

I proceed to the gate, and after verification, I am led inside to a room where other women are already waiting.

The rules are read to us, and then we're given contracts to read and then sign. I skim through it, then sign on the dotted line. So far, I might as well be working at a bank.

We are taken to a changing room to get ready; apparently, the club has different dress codes for different nights. But since it's our first night here, we are to dress in lace and wear masks.

The lady who is helping me dress is a chatterbox; she informs me that tonight everyone, even the men, will be in masks. She then advises me to enjoy my week but not get attached.

"I've seen girls coming here looking for their happily-ever-after, but they end up hurt. You're a pretty little thing—so don't be carried away. Have fun and go home richer, then forget about this place."

To say I'm nervous doesn't cover how I feel. I'm petrified, walking in a state of dream-like panic. And yet part of me is viscerally, even perversely, excited by the experience to come. I follow the other ladies and soon find myself in a vast room filled with people all dressed like me or wearing even less. Velvet, silk, satin, mesh; the room is full of luxurious fabrics and soft skin. The tables are covered with more fabric than the women here, though—myself included. An open-style bar with darkly polished wood and matching high-backed chairs take up most of the room.

There are couches along the walls, and couples are openly kissing, touching each other, and doing more. A girl rests on her knees in front of a man.

I head towards the bar, and even the barman wears a mask. Most club members are dressed in lace, like me, while others are in corsets or leather.

"Uh, excuse me, um…can I have a drink?" I request, feeling badly out of my element.

"You may have one, but you are to address me and all the other men as Sir unless instructed otherwise," he tells me.

"That's presumptuous of you," I scoff under my breath.

"Then you should be wearing leather, not lace," he answers with amusement glinting in his eyes.

Then I spot a bound woman following a guy dressed in brown leather, scrambling on her knees in front of everyone. There is no way in hell I'll ever do that, I vow to myself. How can a grown-ass woman crawl and follow a guy while everyone can see her? I need money, but I can't wrap my mind around crawling after a man for whatever reason. I turn to see the barman waiting patiently.

"Don't tell me that's what is in store for me! I'll see myself out… it's demeaning," I tell him.

"Let me advise you on something important here. If you learn anything tonight, let it be this: never judge something or someone over something you don't understand or even like. Whatever happens in here is consensual. Some people love to be dominated both in and out of the bedroom, while others only enjoy it in the bedroom.

"Here, all fantasies are taken seriously. You see that guy over there? He loves to submit—twenty-four-seven."

I glance over and look away, blushing burgundy. He stares at me knowingly, sets down my drink, and walks off to the other patrons.

I take in the club as I sip my drink. I can see some people dancing in the furthest corner, with slow, sexual music trickling from a masked string quartet and jazz musicians off to the side. There is a lady at the other end giving some guy a blowjob.

Another lady in pink lace joins me. She is more daring, with a thong that covers nothing, but if I had her body, I would flaunt it, too. She looks incredible.

"Why is everyone else in lingerie, too?" she complains. The barman tells her all the new members tonight are wearing lace for easy recognition from other clubgoers.

When she downs her wine in one go and asks for another, a glass of water is all she gets. We learn that only a maximum of two drinks in the space of six hours is allowed at the club.

I decide to take a walk around and pass the time. How am I supposed to remember or identify the men I chatted with? It's not fair that by looking at me, they'll know who I am, and I won't know them.

I mean, almost all the guys are dressed in tight leather that looks great on them. Some of the guys are heavier or short, but it looks as though most people here, whatever their ages, take care of their bodies. There is a mix of people from different backgrounds. A lot of them are white, though, which does make me nervous. Still, I see some brown and golden skin—so perhaps I won't be alone after all. And maybe people won't be judgmental or prejudiced, since they're here to explore their innermost desires anyway…

I round a corner and find the other ladies in lace and a guy explaining domination.

He tells us that domination ranges from fun to a lifestyle, and he hopes by the end of the night, each of us will know what interests us.

He invites us to explore the club and warns against going upstairs.

"The men participating in this week's events are here and will be watching you; if your interests are compatible, then they will approach you. If someone does something you do not like or cannot tolerate, your safe word is red. Mention it once, and a member of our security will be with you shortly, and whatever was happening will come to an abrupt end. Your comfort is of utmost importance, but our Doms will push you out of your comfort zones. They are trained and will know your body better than you do. In short, your happiness and satisfaction lie in their capable hands. They are screened as carefully as yourselves. And now, ladies, let the fun begin!"

Chapter Four

BRYAN

Tonight's events are quite dull; not what I was expecting. First, we have to put on masks; I love seeing a lady's face. All of it, not part of it. How can I enjoy her reactions if her widening eyes are partly concealed? Sure, her body will react, but the eyes hold all the secrets of pleasure and the greatest vulnerability.

My friend and another Dom at the club tell me to stop complaining and look at the upside. We can watch the ladies without their knowledge and then pick the one interested in what we love best.

I head to the bar and find Jim Houston handling the bar. He tells me that I just missed two of the ladies as they went to explore. Out of curiosity, I ask how they were.

"One had this figure, watching her walk is like a dream, with hips meant for holding as I pound into her. The other one looked like a model. But you know me, man, I love them with some meat, something to hold. I love my job, but tonight I wouldn't mind handing it over to someone so I could go explore that lady. Her curves call to the Dom in me."

"Talk to Ben and see if he can take over your job, and then have a go at the lady. Though if I get her before you, I won't be sharing tonight," I tell him as I rise to go and watch the ladies.

The first room has a St. Andrew's cross, and I can see a scene in progress. The lady's pussy is fully visible, and her Dom carefully teases and slaps the tender skin framing her most sensitive area, tracing the whip around her thighs.

I can see her trying to control the situation—to top from the bottom—by the way she is raising her lips in the hope of feeling the whip's sting. She is so wet, it's dripping down her thighs. I can see two of tonight's ladies in lace shift uncomfortably, adjusting their clothes—a clear sign of how turned on they are.

I move to the next room, where another lady is tied down but on a bench this time. Her ass is in the air at an angle that suits the Dom fucking her while another guy eagerly fills her mouth. They are a couple who always come here on Fridays to have a third partner and indulge their exhibitionist urges.

They have drawn quite a crowd, with most of the ladies turned on. I check around and see some other participants closing in and picking the ladies one by one.

I don't know what I'm looking for, but I believe I'll know when I see it. I head back to the dance hall, feeling little hope of meeting a lady who will be worth it tonight. I have become so selective that I'm not even getting laid as much as I used to.

I wish I knew what I'm looking for; then I would pursue it more fervently. But I will rely on instinct until then.

At this moment, a woman in lace catches my eye. Sitting in a secluded corner, she's watching people dance. I move towards her but don't reveal myself. She is seated in a corner, but the lighting is illuminating her, giving out an ethereal quality to her face.

Currently, she is turned away from me, but I can see her flush while watching the dancers. I follow her gaze to see what she's looking for. That's when I notice Madame Selina and her sub dancing; the guy is all over her. Dancing is the only time that sub gets to touch her without permission.

The guy has his hands on her breasts, squeezing them slowly, giving her the tender touch that she always loves. How they manage this relationship, I have never understood, as they work together—with Madam Selina being the company's receptionist, while her sub happens to be the CEO.

I check the other dancers, and that's when I notice what's got the little lady tightening her thighs. The guy is dancing while touching the lady without a care to their surroundings. He then extracts her breast and tongues her nipple, bending forward, while moving his hands between her legs. When the lady throws her head back in ecstasy, my little lady moans.

That moan moves me like nothing else; I have to make her moan my name.

Linnet

After walking around, I'm so turned on that I need to cool off. The lady bent over two men just did me in. It was so hot to watch her take that cock, and I wished I was in her position.

So I go back, and that's when I come across the hidden sofa. Here, I can watch people dance while I cool off, and hopefully by then, all the men will have chosen their ladies. Those women are definitely competing; all I want is for the night to be over so that I can call Nina and find out how Chayla is doing.

That's when I notice a couple dancing, with the guy playing with the lady's breast out in the open. He then presses his hand between her legs, and I can imagine exactly how she's feeling.

I came here for the money, but now I crave a guy like that, someone so hungry for me, he doesn't care where we are. Someone to worship my body. God, watching them is getting me overheated, and I came here to cool down. I can feel how heavy my breasts are, my nipples hardening; I'm glad I'm alone here. They're so hard, this tiny scrap of a bra is hurting them.

What I would give right now to have someone worship them—I would orgasm. That's when I notice I'm no longer alone.

There is a guy in front of me; he kneels before me and asks me to open up. I stare at him without comprehending what he's doing.

"I said, open up. I won't repeat myself." He lifts his eyebrows and waits.

Under his steady gaze, I find myself opening my legs.

"Very nice, baby. I reward good behavior and punish bad behavior. But since it's your first time here, I'll overlook your hesitance."

He inhales my scent, taking in the aroma of my dripping pussy.

"Smells nice. I wonder how it tastes," he tells me as he runs his thumb over my wet lips.

"So wet. Tell me what turns you on more, the idea of him touching her in public, or the possessive way he's doing it?" he asks me, and I don't know what to tell him.

He stops running his finger along my pussy as he waits for my feedback and tells me he wants the truth.

I tell him, "Both."

He pushes my panties to the side and dips a thick finger in my folds. He drags it upward and almost touches my clit. He does this several times, lazily teasing me. I'm about to scream at him to hurry up and rub my clit already. This is real torture. All I want is his finger on my clit, and then at least I'll get some relief.

But he rises to his feet and sits next to me, and I don't know what I'll do to wipe that smirk from his face. He looks like a cat that just ate a canary.

chapter FIVE

I am so pissed at him and decide to finish what he started; I try to take care of myself.

He holds my hand and tells me to try. If I do, I won't like what he'll do to me, he says. Seeing the resolve in his eyes and the way his voice drops an octave, I know it's a losing battle.

He then lifts my breast from my bra and plays with the nipple. He pulls me on his lap and holds me tight while I try to rise.

"What's wrong, baby?" he asks me.

I blurt out, "I'm too heavy."

"In case it's escaped your notice, I like your shape. I love the fact that when I bury my dick so deep in you tonight, I'll have something to hold onto."

Then holding me to him, he wraps his fingers around my thighs and opens them wide.

Nipping my neck, he tells me how he'll bury his hard dick into my softness and watch me squirm as I try to accommodate his cock. He'd do that in front of everyone at the club. "Would you love that? Have everyone watch me claim this beautiful pussy, hear your moans and watch you come apart?"

God, I don't know what's wrong with me, because the idea turns me on so much that I'm panting. I know I'll stain his leather.

Slowly, he starts stroking my calf, and I'm so horny, I try to close my legs and get some relief. But he holds me firmly and warns me never to do that again.

He starts caressing my pussy and lets his fingers to touch my clit… just briefly. It's driving me insane with want, and I find myself begging, "Please."

"Please what, baby?" he asks innocently, continuing his torture.

"Let me come, please."

"You will come when you are ready. As for now, you aren't there yet." Just as he finishes telling me that, the bartender comes and sits across from us.

"Am I interrupting, Master B?" he asks my stranger. Up until now I hadn't even had the thought of asking his name. How sick is it that I want a total stranger to fuck me senseless, and I didn't have the mind to ask even the bare essentials, like his name?

"No, you are not; my girl here likes when someone watches her squirm. Isn't that right, baby girl?"

I wish I could hide and not answer him, but from looking at him and the bartender, without a shadow of a doubt, I know I'll have to answer. Somehow, that's essential to them both.

So I nod, but Master B wants something more, because he stills the fingers that were doing wonders within my pussy—a clear indication that I have to answer verbally.

So for the love of the orgasm that I know is around the corner, I tell them yes.

"Master H, how wet do you think she'll get if I play with her pussy some more?"

"First let me clean her up and see how wet she'll get with proper clit play," the barman answers.

Before I can process what they're up to, Master H gets between our legs, and Master B opens mine wide—wide enough for Master H, who is enormous, to fit between them.

He then licks my folds, and I can't move, since I'm held up tightly by Master B. He tells me, "Don't move or even twitch. Hold still." His hands are a pale contrast on my skin.

He's kissing my neck, his hands playing with my nipples—every touch is driving me crazy. I know I am about to come apart. Master H is just toying with my pussy. Then, as though they've planned it in advance or could read each other's minds, Master H latches onto my clit and sucks hard at the same time that Master B pinches my nipples hard and bites my neck; I come so loud that I'm sure everybody hears my scream.

It takes a few minutes before my breathing is back to normal, and before I can see the smirk on Master H's face. God, what have I done? I want to hide, but Master B tells me how happy he is that I trusted them with my pleasure.

"Seeing you go off like that has made me so hard, but for the next one, you'll come on my cock, and I'll watch you come apart," he tells me as he kisses my neck.

Master H excuses himself and thanks me for letting him taste me. He tells me to let him know later if I need anything at all.

"What he means is, he won't mind making you come again," Master B tells me as we watch Master H go.

I excuse myself to go the ladies' to freshen up, and he gives me three minutes. As I enter the stall and conclude my business, I wonder what he'll do if I am late. With no intention of finding out, I hurry up.

I meet another lady crying outside the stall, and I ask why she's crying.

She tells me it's a long story, but if I'll have a cup of coffee with her, she'll explain.

I forget I had three minutes and soon head to the bar with the woman. Another guy is handling the bar; I request hot chocolate, while my friend asks for coffee with lots of cream.

She tells me her name is Liz, and she came here at the behest of her husband. I asked if the husband is part of the crowd. She tells me no, but his boss is.

I thought it was just a regular competition that I'd participate in and at the end of the week get my money. Liz tells me that her husband got himself in a fix with gambling, and they're at risk of losing everything.

"But I don't think I can do this...this debauchery," she finishes with a hiccup.

"What will you do if you leave now, will your husband be mad at you, where will you get that kind of money?" I ask her.

We chat for a bit before Master H comes and tells me I'm in trouble. Before I can ask him what he means, Master B just picks me up from my stool and ask me whether I still remember my password. I nod to indicate that I'll never forget it.

He stops moving forward and looks expectantly at me.

So I tell him yes, I remember it. He still doesn't move forward but keeps looking at me. I then remember Master H telling me to address the men as 'Sir,' so I tell him, "Yes, sir, I know my password."

He takes me to the room in which I'd seen the lady tied on a bench with two men fucking her. I know everyone can see us, and this turns me on. It shouldn't, but I can't help myself.

"I hope you read your contract before signing; I will discipline you for disobeying your master, who happens to be me. I gave you three minutes, but you didn't get back to me. I had to come looking for you; this is unacceptable. So I'll discipline you and ensure you don't forget the lesson in the future."

"What are you going to do?" I ask him. He opens a cabinet filled with all sorts of punishing tools—whips, canes, and some other things that I've never seen before. My mother used to spank me, but that was nothing. Especially compared to this.

He asks me how many I can take as he approaches me with a paddle. Seven has always been my lucky number, and without thinking, I tell him that.

He takes a seat and asks me to lie across his lap; I can't believe I'm about to be disciplined like a child. So I hesitate, and he tells me he has added two more for my delay, and the longer I take, the more he will add.

I lie across his lap with my ass in the air, visible to everyone watching. I can see my new friend there watching me, as well as Master H. We've gathered a crowd.

Master B then cups my breasts, gaining my full attention.

The crowd recedes, and it's like we're the only two people here. My nipples harden under his probing hands. I can feel the heat from him through my lace, sending up sensations that are wreaking havoc through my body.

I beg him to stop. I apologize and promise to never repeat it, squirming on his lap. I'm aware of his hard hands on me and the thickening cock poking my belly. But the weirdest thing is that I feel safe in his hands—something I haven't felt in ages. I'm confused, hot, and strangely eager for this. Somehow, the best thing I could do would be trusting him.

So that's what I do.

He then tenderly smooths the curves of my ass and tells me that I am ready. Lifting me, he places me on the bench and ties both my knees to the chair. Master B ties my hands, as well. He then adjusts a setting of some sort, and I find my ass raised a bit. All the while, he gently plays with my nipples, caressing the area around them and brushing over them. My body doesn't get the memo that it's about to face some sort of abuse. My nipples just harden, my deepest place getting wet and ready.

I panic for a moment. Should I run? Am I in danger? But I'm turned on, and I can't—and don't want to—move. Today, my body has utterly betrayed me. He presses against my pussy, and a wave of heat flows in my body.

I stop trying to free myself, since there is no give in the ties.

"Hey, baby, it's time to take your punishment. Take it well, and make me happy."

I wonder why I should make him happy. Panic surges up again. I struggle to free myself. A lot of people are laughing.

"I can't wait to make this pretty little ass red. I would love to see you squirm as you sit and remember I did this to you," Bryan tells me softly, caressing my ass. His skin is pale, so stark against mine, like a bone against shadowy ground.

Before I can think of a fitting retort, something hits me. My legs jerk with the sharp pain. I take a breath and vow not to make a sound; I won't give him the satisfaction of crying out. I'll bear the pain with as much dignity as possible, and once he's through, I will leave this place. I'll find the money for Chayla some other way.

The next slap falls on my other cheek, and the pain is the same—sharp and shocking. I can't imagine I have seven more to go. He orders me to count them out.

My butt is on fire, and I'm holding on by a thin thread against crying out. Slaps with the paddle are too much, and soon, I buck against the bench—three more to go. I can't stop tears from leaking from my eyes. *God, what did I involve myself with?*

The next three are so sharp that I yelp on the last one. Once the master is through, I can't help myself, and I sob like a child. He unties me, all the while stroking my back and whispering soft nothings that I can't make out in my current situation. He caresses my back and nipples, and the strangest thing happens: I feel at ease and safe, warmth and pleasure flooding me.

I don't understand what's going on with my body; I just got abused without my consent—though I think that was on the pages of the contract that I skimmed through. But I can feel a loose, soft sensation filling and spreading across my body.

Master B carries me to a sofa, then holds me. We stay like that for what seems like ages.

He runs his hands across my back, up and down, until my breath evens out. When I try to rise, he tightens his hold on me.

Chapter Six

BRYAN

I find an empty sofa and settle on it; I vow to myself not to let her out of my sight again.

I panicked when she hadn't come back, as I had requested. The fear overcame common sense, every other instinct telling me to chill—after all, she is a novice who doesn't know the penalty of disobeying her master.

I went looking for her, only to find she wasn't in the ladies' as I expected. A sweep of the club revealed her at the bar, having a conversation with another new woman. Honestly, I saw red and forgot my training, the admonition to never discipline my sub while in anger.

But her sobs broke my heart. There's no escaping what her tears have done to me.

I have had many subs here at the club, and at one time or another, I have spanked them all.

The pain and shock are usually overcome by their arousal. But even though I can feel by the way her breathing has changed that she's getting aroused, guilt is devouring me.

"It's okay, baby girl."

I wipe away her tears with the pads of my thumb; I shouldn't have punished her as though she was my sub. I feel possessive of her, and I know if I don't step back now, I will have to own her.

But she turns her head and looks at me, her big, beautiful brown eyes filled with sadness. Her lashes are long and dark, like the lovely curls that halo her head. She shudders as she buries her head on my shoulder and gives a choked cry.

I feel it to the depth of my soul—it's too late to step back now. I have found what I've been searching for. Holding her tight, I let my warmth seep in and comfort her. Her shudders have significantly reduced, and I can feel her gearing up for a fight.

She takes a deep breath and tells me she wants to leave.

Panic returns. Maintaining my composure is critical right now. "I will let you leave once I am sure you can stand without assistance; I will take you upstairs and let you relax."

"No, I don't want to be anywhere near you," she tells me in a voice that brooks no argument.

The resistance sends a thrill right down to my cock. I love that she's got a backbone and can stand her ground.

I explain to her that I need her comfort, as well, since I have never disciplined a sub on our first time together. She lets me hold her, and I listen to her heartbeat.

"Let me take you to my room, and I'll prepare a warm bath for you."

"Can't I have some space? I want to be alone right now."

I hate it that she doesn't feel safe with me and offer my room to her. I tell her I won't bother her, but I want to ensure her welfare.

Then her stomach growls, and I take her over to the dining area. By the time she's finished a salmon salad, I can tell she doesn't want to go upstairs and sleep, so I suggest we take a walk around the club.

When we reach the dance floor, I whirl her around, and she shrieks, not expecting it. Her deep, rich laughter warms my heart.

The song is an upbeat one, and we dance. We're good together, and she is a great dancer, but she follows my lead well. When a slow song comes on, I remember how she had watched Madam Selina and her sub with so much longing.

Call me an insensitive jerk if you like, but this is one opportunity that is not going to waste. So I press her to me, and I hear her gasp softly.

I continue dancing, oblivious to the rest of the club. I cup her breasts and fondle them, gauging her reaction. She presses her round, thick ass against me, and I automatically harden. Grinding against her, I let her feel the effect she has on me. Soon, she lets go of her shyness and reveals a wanton side before my eyes.

She throws her head back and arches her back, letting me have unlimited access to her beautiful tits. I press them together; the nipples harden under my hands. Applying some pressure, I pinch them, and I watch how she reacts to the bite of pain I've caused. Then I turn her around and lick them softly, and I can see her melting.

I press my hand against her pussy, and she whimpers. We continue dancing while I play with her body, stroking her thighs and squeezing her ass now and then.

I let her go when I know she's at the edge of coming, and I can see the moment she realizes I've stopped. She's spitting mad, and she is so beautiful when angry, I cannot wait to take her to my room and get rid of that mask.

I want to watch her face as I sink into her softness, watch her as she comes on my cock. She opens her mouth to tell me off, but I kiss her and swallow her words. Kissing her is the best way to shut her up.

The kiss heats up, and I know I have to stop—before I take her right here on the dance floor.

chapter SEVEN

I take her out to the balcony, grabbing two bottles of water as we head out to cool off.

We take seats on a bench and soon realize we're not alone when we hear a moan and some groans.

That's when I see a couple at it—the lady is bending over and taking a thorough pounding. The guy isn't holding back, and I know they will soon come together.

I don't say anything, only watch my pretty sub. Watching her watch the couple is a significant turn-on. She's squirming, pressing her legs together, rubbing those thick, luxurious brown thighs against each other. I have to get between them.

I rise and position myself between her legs. She opens wide without my urging. I lift my face and look at her.

She shrugs and continues watching the couple fuck, her garden absolutely soaking wet before me.

I haven't tasted her yet. I take my first lick, and it's addictive. Fragrant, sweet as wild honey, with a floral scent and her delicious salt. I've never eaten such a sweet pussy before. I lick her clean.

I make sure to neglect her clit; I want her primed for me. I slip a finger into her hot, tight pussy. Going by the way she grips my finger, she's starving for me.

"Will you grip my cock like that when I finally sink into you?" I ask her.

She only gives a soft whimper and moans.

Linnet

I inhale Master B's scent, a mix of spice and pine—he smells delicious and heady.

Despite coming to the balcony to cool off, I can't stop my body temperature from rising.

There's something wrong with me; I shouldn't be getting turned on like this. After this is over, I won't wait three years to get laid; my body has been denied for too long, and now I'm reaping the consequences.

I wish I could squeeze my thighs together and try not to feel how heavy my breasts are. But watching that guy pump into the woman is too hot. I long to be her, to feel what she's experiencing.

To be claimed in such a manner that everyone will know I belong to the guy fucking me senseless.

As he asks me if I'll grip his cock the way I grip his finger, I can't answer. I'm so horny, I might cry if he doesn't fulfill his promise.

He rises and sits next to me, both of us watching the couple as they come together. The lady screams so loud, I am afraid the glass will shatter.

I groan and try to put some distance between us, but his hand shoots out and locks around my waist. It's like a vise—no escape for me.

The ache between my thighs is sharp; it's starting to ache. I need the relief of an orgasm, of penetration. I want to rub my legs together to ease it, but a sixth sense urges me not to try it.

He lifts me quickly to his lap, and I can feel something hard and thick grinding against my ass. It is real torture, and if I survive tonight without screaming in frustration, I'll count that as a win.

I grind myself back against him. Anything that will give me relief is welcome.

He bites my neck, and the sensation is unlike anything I've felt before. I want his fingers on my clit and between my lips, but I know if I push, he'll prolong the torture.

He cups my breasts and rolls the nipples between his fingers. Without letting me know what he's up to, he pinches them hard. The pain is so sharp, I cry out.

The feeling I get is so strong that I'm dripping wet for him. Without conscious thought, I rock my hips back on him. He raises his dick and grinds against me. I know I'll come if we continue like this.

I'm torn between wanting the real thing and being unsure whether I'm allowed to come without his approval. I want to make him happy and try calming down enough to hold my orgasm off.

The arm holding me suddenly lets me go and tears my lingerie babydoll dress in two. My master is like a man possessed; I love it. This powerful side is what I want right now: to be controlled. For a man to want me so much, it overwhelms him. It calls to something ancient, that interplay of power and pleasure that goes back through humanity for thousands of years: a visceral drive to fuck and be fucked.

When he uses his fingers to spread me fully, I can't control the whimper that escapes my mouth.

He finally touches my clit, and I go off like a rocket. I come with a scream, and before I know it, he flips me and bends me over the bench.

I knew the guy was well-built, but he just flipped me over like I weighed nothing. And I'm a thick, fleshy woman. His strength is so damn hot.

He rests his cock against my entrance. I want him so much. The head of his cock presses against my sensitive, juicy lips. I arch my back and give him a better angle. He enters me in one stroke, and it's uncomfortable at first.

Taking a deep breath, I loosen my muscles to accommodate him. I'm so full of his dick, and it feels great. It's precisely what I've been missing, and I needed this: to be ravished by a man who knows what I want.

He tells me to hold onto the bench and not let go.

"It's going to be a rough ride, darling. I'll take you gently later. For now, this is mine."

Pulling back almost to the tip, he slides in slowly. I'm wondering how this is rough; I'm ready for a hard ride. He does this twice, then he ups his game. He slams in so hard, I'm afraid if I let go, I'll be thrown to the other side of the balcony. I hold on for dear life.

After some time, I start meeting his thrusts, and we lose ourselves in the sensations. I come once again, and I can feel my pussy gripping his cock.

"That's it, baby. Don't let go of my cock. I'm going to fuck you so good. I want you addicted to my cock," he says, slamming into me.

I'm having spasms, holding him tight with my walls. He slams faster and harder. He has lost control, and another orgasm is rising in me. I know it will take me to another level, but I want it, and so I raise my ass higher and meet him thrust for thrust.

I come in a way that I've never thought possible; I can feel the waves in every part of my body. At the back of my mind, I hear him roar as he comes, but I am beyond anything.

He collapses on top of me, and I welcome his weight. I feel right at home.

I know he has just destroyed me for other men. No man will ever top what we just had. We take several minutes to catch our breath. He lifts me, and in doing so, my mask comes off.

By now, the party has been taken to the private suites upstairs. Someone switches the balcony lights back to normal, overpowering the dim sconce lighting.

chapter EIGHT

"Lynn? What the fuck!" Master B exclaims.

Wait a minute—how does he even know my name? I don't remember giving it to him, and he never asked. Only friends call me Lynn; even workmates call me Linnet.

"Um...how do you know my name?" I ask him.

"So, it's you?"

"Who are you?" I ask him. I want to keep my private life separate from...this, whatever this is.

He then removes his mask, and I wish the world would swallow me whole. I close my eyes and hope when I finally open them, it will have been a hallucination.

I know fate hates me, but this is too much. My world just got rocked by my husband's brother. And what's more—a husband from whom I never got to file for divorce, and who has never contacted me. I was afraid if he knew about Chayla, he would take her away.

Looking at Bryan's face, I can feel him closing himself off from me. He's spitting mad.

"So, this is why you left my younger brother? Wasn't he kinky enough for you?" he asks me with a voice full of contempt.

"Bryan…"

"What? Don't you dare call me by my name. You haven't earned the right to do so," he growls at me in warning

Gone is the man who made me feel something real for the first time in my miserable life.

So I take a deep breath, rise with as much dignity as I can, and leave.

My legs are not yet steady, and I grab at the nearby railings as I try to get my bearings back.

Then I'm lifted and carried in a fireman's hold. I kick, and when I think of screaming, he tells me to try it—but know I'll regret it later.

BRYAN

I can't believe I fucked my brother's wife. Mike is my younger stepbrother, whom I have a love-hate relationship with, but no matter what, I know he has my back.

When his wife just up and left him, he fell apart. He came to see me. We searched everywhere from New York to Austin. They had a cabin in the mountains, but even there, we couldn't find her.

After six months with nothing, our family encouraged Mike to move on. He's found someone and has been dating her for the last two years. He even moved in with his new girlfriend. I know Mike wants to settle down with Clarice as soon as possible. The only hitch was the missing wife—who just landed in my lap. Literally.

The shock of finding her here is wearing off. I know I've been harsh on her. But I can't just let her go.

I can't explain this connection between us. She always caught my eye on the rare occasions Mike actually brought her around, but now…to hell with it. I can't explain how I feel, but I know we fit. We were meant to be.

She is mine. I've just claimed her, and I take care of what is mine.

I'll sort Mike out later. Right now, I have a sub to worship all night long. By the end of this week, she will be mine in every sense. She's the one I've been searching for all along.

I always take what I want, and to hell with anyone who's uncomfortable with my decisions.

She tries to leave, but with such unsteady legs, it's a task that she can't manage. I wouldn't let her go even if she could walk straight. I pick her up and hoist her over my shoulders; I don't care what she thinks. I'll set her straight within no time. I mumble some inane warning, and she goes quiet quickly.

I bathe her, and she is reticent, though speaking volumes with her eyes. But I am content for now.

"It's past one o'clock. We will sleep and talk in the morning," I tell her, lying down with her in my arms.

Soon she closes her eyes, and I can feel how even her breaths are. Only then do I sleep.

When I wake up, it's to the soft snoring of my angel. I take time watching her sleep without a care in the world and wonder what brought her to the club and the competition.

There are two types of women who participate in the quarterly club competition. One group is for women who want the cash at the end of the week. The other is the group that wants an inroad to the lifestyle. Lynn doesn't fit into the second group, and if it's the money, then all she had to do was get a divorce from my brother. The settlement would have been more than what she could possibly make here.

I start tracing her cheeks; I always loved the way her brown skin looked tanned, no matter the season.

When Mike married her in Vegas, he brought her to Mama in Austin. She was shy and very self-conscious.

I can still see that girl in the woman in my arms. Soon, I'm tracing my hands over her sensitive breasts, and can't wait for her to wake up so that I can have my fill.

But as I trace my way down, I see a caesarian section line. So, my little sub is a mother. As a doctor, I would know that scar anywhere. Will she trust me enough and let me know what's compelled her to come here? As I trace the scar, I notice her breathing has changed, and I know she is awake.

I continue my exploration and wait to see how long she will pretend to be asleep.

As I trace her inner thighs, she opens them discreetly. I pretend that I don't notice the invitation to explore further. My cock is now at full mast, and I know I'll have her before we can have any meaningful conversation.

Usually, my control is top-notch, but with her, I'm almost helpless. I grind against her ass, and she rocks back. I press my head against her pussy, and she moans.

"I know you're not asleep, and I have two questions before I take you," I whisper into her ear.

"I expect nothing but the truth, Linnet. Nod if you understand,"

She nods her head.

She's so wet, and very responsive to me. I've never taken drugs, but Linnet has just become my new addiction. I want her with an intensity that worries even me.

chapter NINE

Every time I touch her, especially now that I have my dick bathed in her essence, I can't help but obey the electric sensations. I've never felt so much, so strongly, in my life.

I hold her still; she's writhing, wanting more of my cock. She'll have it, but I need to rein in my desires for her, or else I'll shoot as soon as I get into her tight pussy.

This pussy is mine. She may not know it, but I'm going to possess her utterly. She is mine, and her place is next to me, in my bed.

She's very close, and I don't want her to come before me. This time, we will come together—whether she wants to or not. I sink my teeth on her neck, giving her a painful nip, something to ground her.

She lets out a low groan when I skim over her clit. I can feel her frustration when I stop moving my fingers; she's a greedy sub. Precisely what I want in a woman: someone who loves sex as much as I do.

She begs me to let her come, but I hold steadfast and I still my raging cock. All my blood has gone south, and my cock is throbbing with pain. Not the best state to be in, especially when

I have a willing woman in my arms, but I have to show her that I control her orgasms.

She will come when I want her to come—and have the ride of a lifetime.

"How long since you last got laid, Linnet?"

I hold her still and wait for her answer. I know it's been a while, since her body can't lie, but I need to hear it from her lips.

She doesn't answer right away, and I grip her harder, a firm reminder that I expect nothing but the truth.

"Linnet...I won't repeat myself. How long has it been since you had a dick inside this pussy?" I ask her softly. I know she won't mistake the softness in my voice for anything else.

"You won't believe me if I answer correctly," she whispers—so softly that if I weren't listening, I wouldn't have heard her.

"Try me."

"More than three years. The last guy who had me was your brother Mike."

I can hear the genuineness in her voice, and even if I have my reservations, I let them go in favor of my second question. "Are you on contraceptives?"

The moment I hear her say, "no," I thrust home, filling her. I pause for a moment to let her adjust to my width. I have a big cock, and I know how to use it.

I promised her some gentle lovemaking, but I'll do that later. Right now, there is something unbelievable about having her like this. I know it is against the club rules, but I'm possessed.

If Arthur finds out I took her without a condom, he might even suspend my membership. But I can do without the club now that I've found what I've searched for all along.

Knowing she's open for me and will take anything I give her makes me feral, and I fuck her in wild abandon. I slam in hard, pull out to the tip, and then slam in again. Within a few minutes, I can feel a tingling sensation at the base of my spine, and I know I'll come, exploding. I ask her to go as I increase my thrust. She blows all around me, and feeling her hotness surrounding me makes me come immediately.

"That's good; you won't need them 'til you have my children in you," I tell her.

"I never knew you were nuts. You were always the brains of the family. Do any of them know how crazy you are?" she asks.

I always loved her sense of humor, and I let her know it.

Linnet

I can't believe I woke up to Bryan caressing me, and I couldn't control how much I wanted him. This man has given me the most powerful orgasms that I've ever had in my life.

I don't know how I'll survive after this week. The guilt and regret will finish me off.

I felt ashamed when he asked me how long it has been. I was tempted to lie to him, but when he growled in that sexy voice of his, I knew I had to tell the truth.

Whether he believed or not is a non-issue for me. I will go with the flow, enjoy the week, and, in the end, have enough cash to cover my baby girl's medical bills. Nothing could be better than that.

We have to have the talk he promised me last night, and I'm dreading it. If he goes all Dom on me, I'll have to tell him about Chayla.

Yet despite that, with Bryan, I don't feel threatened. I can't even believe I'm entertaining the idea of coming clean with him.

He makes me feel comfortable, but I have to put my girl first. She always goes above everything else. I want her to have the love I never had. But am I denying her something by keeping her away from Mike and his family?

They are the only family she has—after all, I broke ties with mine when I moved away from home. Life in that tiny town was unbearable. I was an outsider. My stepmom claimed I was an ungrateful brat, and everybody else treated me accordingly. Why endure the torture of living in a place like that? Nothing I could have said would have changed the way my mother treated me—and it's not like she gave me an example that made others seem trustworthy, either.

Bryan tells me to take a shower while he makes some calls. "Make it quick, or I'll come for you, and I don't think you're ready for me right now," he adds, his eyes hooded.

When I'm finished in the shower, we get room service, and I can feel Bryan's gaze on me.

"What, can't I have breakfast in peace?" I ask him.

"You know what I want from you," he tells me.

"Just humor me. What exactly do you want to know?" I Bryan knows I'm stalling, but I can't help it—I'm nervous.

"I want to know why you left my brother and where you've been, for starters," he tells me. I can see he is curious and genuine in concern, rather than merely angry.

I tell him how his brother betrayed me and why I left. I skim over my life for the last three years.

He sees through me and tells me so.

"Let's get something straight, Linnet; I am your Dom, whether you like it or not. I want nothing but the truth from you, not something I can gather from your Facebook page. Don't let it happen again. Any time I ask you a question, I expect the truth, and nothing else. You can trust me. I won't hurt you," Bryan assures me.

"Look, Bryan, it's not that I don't trust you. Some things are best suited to stay in the past. After the week is over, I want us to go our separate ways with no regrets and hard feelings. The truth is that your brother hurt me, and I left to lick my wounds. Then I moved on. That's life," I tell him.

"Linnet…"

"Okay, but don't judge me. I did what I felt was right. When Mike betrayed me with his secretary, it was so painful."

"Who told you that? Did they have any proof of his cheating?"

"Nobody told me. I caught them in the study, with her giving him a blowjob. I had left classes early, since I knew he was working from home. I didn't call beforehand; I wanted to surprise him. But I got a surprise that changed my life forever. I couldn't even look at him after that."

"I'm sorry. Truly, I am. But I can see there's more you're not telling me."

"Come on, Bryan, it's water under the bridge now," I tell him.

He looks at me, then picks his phone from the table.

I think he is going to call his brother, but he told me to trust him not to hurt me. I decide to wait and see.

chapter TEN

"Hello, this is Doctor Payne. Is Mr. Warren in the office?" he asks someone on the other line.

"Thank you...Warren, how are you? No... I'm fine; everyone is fine. I want to hire you to get me some information that I urgently need. Yes. No, nothing like that. I know you deal with the company's issues, but this is very important to me. It's personal."

My face heats as I figure out what he's up to. I snatch his phone and end the call. "What are you doing, Bryan? You want to hire a PI on me?"

"Linnet, I'm a busy man who gets what he wants—one way or another. I want the truth—either from you or from a PI; it doesn't matter. So give me back my phone so that I can resume my call. Or are you finally going to tell me what you're hiding?"

With nothing else to lose, I tell him of confirming my pregnancy at the school and rushing home to share the news with my husband—only to find his secretary between his thighs.

"Then where did you go?" he asks me.

"I stayed with my friend Nina for a couple of weeks, and then moved into a hostel, but after the semester was over, I moved to Kansas City."

"Why Kansas? You could have come here. Not to brag, but we've got the best doctors. Plus, Mama is here, and she would have taken care of you."

"I just wanted a fresh start, and Nina's mother has always been like my own. I don't really have a family. So I recuperated with her and had my baby there."

"Then what happened to my niece or nephew?"

"You would have made a great detective, you know."

"Lynn, stop stalling," he growls at me. It's like he knows all my tricks already. Well, he should—not that I knew Bryan well when Mike and I were together, mind you.

"You have a niece, and no, Mike doesn't know about her. I have moved on with life, and I want to forget the past, while focusing on the future."

"Go on. What happened next? Just let me have the story. I'll ask questions later. I have several, and we have the next six days, if that's the way you want to do it."

I can feel his displeasure, and I don't know why, but I want to make him happy with me. I want to please him—something that I've never wanted with anybody else.

So I tell him how I left Kansas and went back to New York. How I tried working with a young one while I took night classes. I was unable to make ends meet and had to move back to Austin when I lost my job in New York. Then a friend offered me a job here.

Then I tell him about my daughter's condition, how I have finally learned that she has a heart abnormality requiring surgery as soon as possible. I hate that I can't do this without breaking down. I'm the kind of woman who keeps it together—always. He holds me close, and I sob until I'm calm.

"So that's why you're here at the club?" he asks me.

I nod.

"Why didn't you come to me? I could have organized and assisted with my niece's medical care. Ensured she gets the best. You've been here for the last two years, maybe an hour from Mom's place, and haven't let her meet her first grandchild? That's cruel of you, Linnet, and honestly, I didn't expect this from you. I'm trying to understand you—but why not come to us?

What if you had met some of the more sadistic members of the club?"

I know where he's coming from, but it hurts to hear the censure in his voice. But I had gone through enough rejection. Subjecting my daughter to it wasn't something I was willing to do. If they hadn't helped us, then I would have wasted effort and my pride, and again—what if Mike had tried to get full custody? They have the money, and—I hate to say it—certain advantages. A Black woman trying to keep her child is going to have less luck than a white father, and that's just how it is.

The club was my best bet; it still is. With the money I'll get at the end of the week, I'll find her the best cardiologist possible, then move on.

Bryan

"Tell me about your upbringing," I ask Linnet abruptly, feeling the pain in her voice as she tells me that she didn't want to subject her daughter to rejection. I am perceptive, and I know someone hurt her enough that she doesn't expect any kindness from us or anybody else.

She slowly opens up about her childhood and her stepmother's treatment. It pulls at my heartstrings. I can seldom speak this easily on such a personal level, but with Linnet, it comes pouring out.

I was in her position when I lost my mother to cancer, but the woman my father married stepped in.

Mama—as she likes people to call her—loves me as much as she loves her kids, and I have never felt any different. She took me as her own and gave me unconditional love, even after she had Mike and later, Shelly; I was always her first child.

I can't fathom having lost a mother and a father at the same time, then putting up with a vindictive stepmother. But I know Mama will feel slighted that Linnet didn't trust her enough to let her meet her granddaughter.

"I wish the club could allow us out before the weekend so that I can check on her. What's her name?" I ask her.

"She's Chayla Brookes Payne," she answers me shyly.

"You named her after Mama? That will save you some scolding," I tell her, allowing a smile to cross my lips.

"After her and Nina's mother, too. Those women have been the mothers I never had. I'm sorry I didn't let you into Chayla's life, but she's all I have. Please don't let Mike take her from me," she implores me. I can see the raw fear in her eyes, and it breaks me.

I tilt her chin up and make eye contact because I want her to see the sincerity in my eyes. "Lynn, do you remember what happened last night? Has anything like that ever happened to you before?" I wait for her answer, and when she answers with negation, I continue and tell her that she's mine now.

I have never felt it before, either, and I have no intention of letting go of the best thing that has happened to me. But I'll need to show her with actions instead of just telling her. I know what the brotherhood will expect when I come clean.

I'm not yet ready, but it will have to do. When I joined the club, it was with six of my friends. We are successful in our fields, and when one decides to settle with a woman, the brotherhood has to approve the match.

But that will come later. First, my niece needs to be taken care of. I make arrangements to have Chayla's file sent to my office and another copy sent to my email.

I don't want to rush her, but I always take instantaneous action whenever I want something done. Taking over her life is the last thing I want to do, but after the week is over, she will be at my house, living there with my niece.

Once she finds out that I have requested Chayla's file, she asks me why. I tell her that in our family, we stick together, and that's what we will do. I leave her to talk to her friend in private as I make a call.

My brother knows about the club, but what he doesn't know is that I am here with his soon-to-be ex-wife. I tell him I'm at the club, and if he could have them sent over, I have a way for him to get divorce papers for Linnet.

chapter ELEVEN

"Bryan, I can take care of myself and my daughter. I know you mean well, but this is something that I have to do on my own."

I know we're going to have some issues if I don't set her straight. In my world, my word is law.

I take my shirt off and turn to go to the bathroom, and she gasps. "You've got tattoos? How come I've never seen them? Can I look?"

She is so excited that I find myself grinning. I always wanted to get some, but with my profession, it didn't feel right. The club opened my mind up. Now I do what makes me happy, and to hell with the people who aren't comfortable with it.

"You like? I'll let you near them after your bath," I tell her as I draw the water. I want her to enjoy the calm before the storm.

Once I tell the brotherhood that I've claimed her, we'll have to perform a mating ceremony. Yes, a mating ceremony. Ben is such an ass. He came up with that term, but it stuck.

These men will always have my back. I never thought I would go through the ceremony. My woman also has to go through training.

Our union will have to survive until we breathe our last; divorce is not an option. Marriage is forever. However, I've seen others who are united or married being happy.

I want to take some time and prepare her for the upcoming ceremony, so I've rushed her bath. If I don't hurry, someone will watch the tape and see that I claimed her last night, and I don't want that. I like things done at my own pace—as soon as possible, sure, but on my terms.

I towel-dry Lynn and carry her to bed, and I notice she's trying to read the minute script emblazoned across on my chest.

Her soft fingers stroking my pectorals are driving me insane. I hold her hands still, and that makes her look at me. "There's something I need you to know. Last night I took and claimed you as my own. That's a vow that only death can break."

Lynn looks alarmed and annoyed. "But Bryan, you can't promise something like that. We might not be compatible. Why don't we try to date at first? If we find we're okay down the line, then maybe we can think of something permanent," she tells me.

"Nope, that's not gonna happen," I tell her, kissing her neck. "You're mine now, and I must let the club…" Before I can finish my sentence, I'm interrupted by a knock at the door.

I know my time is up; I hope the lesson I taught her last night about obedience is still fresh in her mind.

"Come in," I tell whoever is at the door, still caressing her. I know she's horny, but my plan to worship her body is officially on hold for now.

Ben comes in and takes a seat without waiting to be asked. If he wants to play that game, I'll oblige him.

I don't say anything as I trail my fingers down to my woman's center. She is drenched already, excited just by having Ben in the room.

She's in for a shock; by the time the week is over, she won't recognize herself. I insert two digits at once, and she moans. I slowly thrust in and out of her as I wait for Ben to tell me why he's in my suite.

Ben is a voyeur, so he enjoys the show without saying anything. When I move to her nipple and take the little nub in my mouth and start sucking, he finally tells me that Arthur wants me in the study.

Nothing new. I expected the sermons, which means my girl will have to wait a little bit longer to have her orgasm. I withdraw my digits from her channel, and she whimpers.

I put one finger near her mouth, and she opens up. She sucks it so well that I might come just watching her. She knows she's got me, and she's enjoying it.

I remove my finger from her mouth, and she pouts. I'll have to deal with her later. Watching her, I clean my other finger with my tongue.

I raise her chin so that I can talk to her, and she can see my eyes, because what I am telling her is crucial. "Don't leave this room under any circumstances, do you understand me? Unless the building is on fire, stay here. I'll come back to finish what I have started. And Lynn, I want you to trust me completely. No questions asked. Whatever will happen is meant to be. I've got your back, so make sure you have mine, too."

LINNET

I don't know what just happened, but Ben's arrival has changed something. I have this feeling that whatever comes next, I won't like it—but deep inside, I know I can't let Bryan down.

He looked so vulnerable when he asked me to trust him and to have his back. I still wish I could make out the writing on his chest; it somehow looked important. Unlike the tribal pattern on his upper arm, the chest tattoo was much more intricate.

As I lie here in bed, I think about our past together. In truth, this isn't the start. Back when Mike introduced us—a brief time, admittedly; I spent more time with the boys' parents—I was always interested in Bryan. I loved the way he could command a room whenever he entered. At the time, though, I thought it was because he was the eldest, having the mantle of leadership for their family.

Then he picked up his aunt's company and managed it into fame and success. With his reputation as a prominent surgeon, too, he was out of my league. What could a nurse-in-training have to offer a multi-millionaire physician? Sure, we both had type-A personalities, but that didn't mean I was on his level. Mike, for his part, seemed awestruck by his big brother—and whenever he saw my reaction to Bryan's presence, Mike was jealous.

It's going to be tricky. Part of me is gleeful and elated to have this chance with Bryan, but my practical side is full of doubts.

I wish there were a way we could be together after this. I know he says that I'm his, but I don't know precisely what it means. But it would be nice to have someone I can always count on when I need to. I've always been alone, and often lonely—but I'm used to being let down and abandoned, or just not having my needs met. I'd like to think things could be different here, but I'm pretty dubious.

Mike was my friend, but our relationship lacked passion. After letting go of the anger, I can now see why our marriage was tepid. I can't believe these men are related; Mike would never even allow me to suck his cock. He always saw me as fragile, made of glass. He cared, sure, but he underestimated me and was always gingerly with me.

What Bryan gave me last night is something I have always desired. I can't even imagine being with another man the same way. My stepmother was right—I always want what I can never have.

This week is going to be special, and I'll have the memories to carry me down the line. Whatever Bryan has done to me, nothing can undo it. I want more of this.

Maybe I can make this club thing work after all. Although after him, anyone else is sure to be a let-down…

To take my mind off what's going on, I take a look around the suite. We have a bedroom with a small kitchenette attached to it. Next to the bed, there are some drawers, and out of curiosity, I start opening them.

There are so many toys— I don't even know how some of them are used. But I can identify dildos in all sizes and colors. I had seen butt plugs at Nina's, but the purpose of that three-pronged thing? I have no idea. The rest? I can only guess.

I pick up a beautiful necklace of some sort, wondering at its design, when the door suddenly opens.

Thinking it's Bryan, I ask him if he would mind showing me how to put on the necklace.

I turn and see the guy who'd been whipping a lady at the party last night. Shocked, I drop the necklace, which he picks up quickly.

"Definitely, doll. There's nothing I would like more than to put it on you. The diamonds would complement you just right."

He rips my towel off and cups my breasts. I try to move his hands, but it's like pushing a wall.

"Come on; I promise I'll only put the chain on you—nothing else," he assures me.

Before I can tell him off, he has me on my back on the bed and sucks my nipple into his mouth, while his other hand pinches my other nipple.

The pain goes directly to my core, and it starts throbbing again. I try squeezing my legs together, but he won't let me.

He clips one diamond end on my nipple, and I scream. The pain is sharp and unexpected.

"Your necklace has three diamonds. Can you guess where the other two will go?" he asks me, with a smile that shows off beautiful dimples.

"This isn't a necklace, is it?" I ask him. The pain has reduced, and I can feel how tender my breast is.

He sucks the other breast, and I now know what to expect. I try moving away from him before he can clamp my other nipple, but the guy is fast. Within no time, both my breasts are trapped by the clips. I hadn't noticed them before—I thought they were some sort of clasp, and they're hidden behind clusters of rhinestones.

"You look beautiful with the nipple clips on. But no, it's not a necklace."

"You could have *told* me it was not a necklace instead of this," I tell him, pointing at my chest.

"I believe in teaching through example; that way, the lesson sticks. Besides, I always indulge a lady," he tells me, then bends and takes my aching clit in his mouth.

One hard suck, and I come hard. But before my orgasm is over, he clips my clit. The pain is like nothing I've ever experienced. He kisses me, and the strangest thing happens. My clit starts pulsing with arousal. Every breath I take jiggles my tits, and the motion goes directly to my clit.

I can't imagine being turned on with a stranger watching me. What will Bryan think? I try to sit, but my clit throbs too much.

"I wish I could ease your throbbing clit, but Bryan would kill me…so let's get you downstairs with the others," he tells me, then tries to pick me up.

I remember Bryan told me not to leave the room under any circumstances. So I tell him I can't go with him, but I'll join the others downstairs when Bryan gets back.

"So, how do you suggest we pass the time 'til your master joins us?" he asks me.

"Go ahead and join the others. I promise I'll come downstairs with Bryan," I urge, trying to get him to leave.

The nipple clamps are wreaking havoc on my control, and I know I won't be in a position to stop him if he tries to take me. Would it jeopardize what I have with Bryan? I don't want to find out. Yes, he let Master H lick me. And then again, he didn't seem to mind while he was watching him finger me earlier.

But would he mind if he found another master with me in his absence? Would he share me with others? For that matter, would I allow him to do that to me?

God, my head is rolling, and the ache between my legs isn't helping me. I try counting from a thousand backward, hoping to reduce the pain.

"You know I can help you come again. Just say the word."

"No, I'll wait for Bryan; he won't take long."

chapter TWELVE

BRYAN

Once I'm outside, Ben hits my shoulder and laughs.

"What?"

"You're one mean motherfucker. You could have let her come. I could have waited and enjoyed watching her explode."

"Look, Ben, I want to be done with Arthur so that I can take care of my lady properly."

"You're the last guy I expected to fall, but I assure you, I'll enjoy the ceremony."

"Your time will come, too, and I'll get to pay you back," I retort as we enter the study.

"Well, well...took you long enough to get here," Arthur tells me as he rises from his chair and goes to the open window.

"I was busy," I tell him. Ben lights up a cigarette.

"Fill me in on your mate. What you know about her? Do we need to get Clerk involved?"

I know the club means well. They've run a background check on the girls before, but now that I've claimed one, they need to be sure about her.

To save on time, I tell Arthur and Ben about Linnet and how I know her—the whole truth.

"So, in short, you're fucking your brother's wife? Then you can't claim her until she's divorced," Arthur tells me.

"I asked my brother to send over the divorce papers, which I expect any moment now; he has moved on and is staying with his current girlfriend."

"Call again and ask how long they'll be. We can't perform the rites until he does."

I call Mike and put him on the speaker. He's out of the state, but he assures me that once he gets back, he'll send them over.

Arthur says that since he's heard from my brother, he will talk with Linnet, and if she's ready to sign the divorce papers herself, then we can perform the rituals.

"She should be downstairs with the other ladies. Let's go get her."

I tell Arthur that she's in my suite, where I left her. He tells me that he sent Cormack to take her downstairs to join the rest.

He decides to watch the feed to my suite, and that's when I see Cormack enter.

What follows gets my blood boiling. Cormack had no right whatsoever to put his hands on her. He is smart enough that I can't fault him. But what hurts most is that she lets him.

But seeing her in the throes of a near-orgasm that I didn't authorize makes me see red.

I can see both Arthur and Ben are enjoying this; I'm not. I turn to leave, but Arthur says I can't, I have to sit back and watch. To see how loyal she is, and how far she'll go.

"Make this a test to see if she learned anything last night. Learn from the mistakes you've made so far. Does she know that she can come only when you approve? Have you laid down any rules? If not, you've failed her. Remember, a good Dom takes care of his sub by ensuring she knows what you expect and what will happen when she doesn't meet your expectations.

"Yes, Cormack took advantage of the situation, but I think he's messing with you. If he wanted to have her, he would have, because that girl is not in a position to safe-word. Go and teach her a lesson she won't forget, and meet us upstairs in thirty minutes. Everything should be ready by then. And Bryan, you will only watch until she does her training."

As I leave the study, I take the long way back to my suite. I don't want to face Cormack with my anger; I know why he did what he did. He was paying me back for fucking his girl without his consent last year. But I didn't realize that the girl was his; she never said. I apologized—but he knew damn well that I had claimed Linnet.

If I can remove my emotions, then maybe I can look at the situation in a different light. By the time I get to my suite, I have my feelings well under control, but I can't trust myself with Linnet.

Cormack is seated on the same chair Ben had taken earlier, while Lynn is lying on the bed. If I didn't know better, I would say she's in pain. She is panting too much, which isn't helping her at all. The more she does that, the more it will vibrate her clit.

"I can see you're uncomfortable. Since you're new to this; I am going to be lenient with you," I tell her as I clean my hands. I ask Cormack to leave, since he isn't needed.

"Look, Bryan, I'm sorry. I shouldn't have touched her without your permission," he tells me as he leaves.

My anger dies with his admission; I know he means what he says.

I take a butt plug from the drawer and hand it to him; it's my way of extending an olive branch—and to teach Lynn a lesson she won't forget in the future.

She is so drenched, Cormack merely runs the small plug through her juices and then inserts it in her ass. She tries to block his hand, but one look from me makes her relent.

Once the butt plug is in her, I switch it to a low speed. Cormack looks at me for direction, and with my nod, he takes his place between her thighs.

He pleasures her using one finger; I watch as she tries to stave off the orgasm, to no avail. I start playing with the nipple clamps, knowing the effects are converging on her clit.

She screams as she comes, and I wait until she is coherent enough to tell her that all her orgasms will be under my command.

"You ever make the same mistake again, you won't like what I'll do to you," I promise her, and I know by the look on her face, she realizes how serious I am.

Cormack leaves us, without letting her know what I want to do. I leave her alone and head to the bathroom, then start running a bath. Once the clamps come off, she will be in some pain. The shower will ease it; that's all I can do for her.

Once I get back, I remove the clamps and soothe the nipples immediately. She comes every time I remove a clip.

By the end of the day, her body will be wrung out. She is so responsive, and I'm happy to have her. But will she hate me by the end of it?

One thing I'm sure of is that she's mine, and nobody—even herself—is going to keep me from her.

I take her to the tub and wash her gently. By the time I reach her pussy, she's wet once again. I know I shouldn't take her, but when it comes to her, I have no control.

I carry her to the bed, spread her legs, and enter her slowly. I watch her gaze at my dick as I move forward, inch by inch. We are running late, and I don't want to fuck her—I want to make love to her before all the madness starts.

I can't have her until all my brothers make her come, so it's my way of letting her know how much I treasure her. I have participated in the last three rites of my brothers' mates and ensured they learned what we thought was necessary for them to be happy. During the ceremony, I never knew how hard it must have been for them.

It's killing me that I have to share her, and not knowing what they have planned for her is murder. But it's only for this one time. I know she'll be allowed to have any man she wants once we're mates—but only with my consent.

And that's something I know I'll never give her after this.

I take her gently and show her how I feel, and soon, she's crying. I wipe away her tears and increase the rhythm. For the first time, we come in a shared, intense moment.

I dress her in a gown and make sure she has put on a thong. I don't wipe away or clean up the scent of our lovemaking—I want those assholes to smell me on her and know that she's mine.

chapter THIRTEEN

I can't feel my limbs, I'm so tired; I hope Bryan will let me sleep. He was barely controlling his anger earlier.

This place has taken me on an emotional rollercoaster. I feel like I've lost all control over my body.

Once we get settled, I am going to talk to him. As seductive and delicious as this experience has been, I'm thoroughly annoyed at Bryan. Getting angry at me for something that was beyond my control is unfair.

Then there's the issue of him controlling my orgasms. Who the hell does he think he is? I'll get a vibrator and some of those toys I saw, and I will be fine.

We get into the elevator, and soon, we are on the highest floor. The security here is tight, and we get in only after Bryan has entered several passwords and codes.

Then we're in a room full of men—most of whom I saw around the club last night. It seems like eons ago. Master A welcomes us in a booming voice.

Then a tiny lady comes from the other side of the room and asks Bryan if it's okay for her to take me into the kitchen. Having another woman here makes me feel a lot better; I didn't know how apprehensive I was until this dainty woman dragged me away.

Once we are away from the men, I blurt out, "Was that Senator Briggs back there?"

"Come on, I'll introduce you to the other girls in this hellhole. But you'll love it as much as we do," she tells me.

She's excited, but all I want is to lock myself in my room and think everything over. I like having an organized life, having a plan, and this place is just chaotic. I have basically no agency. And yet it's seductive and overwhelming…I have no idea how to process it all.

The other ladies are seated on the kitchen island. My rescuer introduces herself as Jessica.

Another woman says, "Hi, I'm Sue, and Cormack is my husband."

I'm shocked. How will she react when she finds out what I did? "I…I…I didn't know he was married earlier…" Before I finish stammering my half-assed apology, they all laugh.

These women must be just as nuts as the men in the other room.

Jessica tells me not to worry; anything goes during the mating season.

"Mating season?" I ask her.

They look at each other and then back at me like I am the biggest idiot they've ever met. Then Merinda, who is Senator Briggs's wife, asks me what Bryan has told me.

I tell them he's explained nothing; all I know is that he was acting strange earlier.

"He didn't promise you anything this morning?" she asks me, with visible pity.

I hate being pitied by anyone over anything. Before I can answer her, Sue tells me to think back over anything that Bryan has said to me since last night.

"Just something about me being his or something."

Now they're looking at me like I've won the lottery. I thought I was going to be involved in some kind of draw, or raffle, but that's fallen by the wayside. It seems like having Bryan claim me has completely taken me out of the running. All that, after I had to chat with some of these guys and get their various propositions? Well, I suppose Bryan must be important because people seem willing to break rules or change things when he's involved. But everyone's still excited about my presence here, and they all seem keen on having fresh meat to play with.

I'm still not sure how I feel about being that meat. And for that matter—what about Chayla's surgery? I still have to pay for it somehow…I'm so far from what I intended here, and I can't help feeling guilty about that. But maybe I can get help from the club somehow…there's certainly enough members for it.

Merinda takes over and tells me that the club has several brotherhoods, and that each brotherhood has seven members.

"My husband and Bryan belong to one, and when a member decides to settle down with one woman, the brotherhood conducts a rite that unites the couple and the brotherhood. So that's why we're all here to witness your union with Bryan."

"So, what will happen? Are we going to say vows or something?"

"I can't say precisely what will happen; the ceremony usually varies. But one consistent thing is that the guy who's your mate will have your name tattooed on his back.

"When I got mated, I was tied up, and every guy there made me come. God, I can still feel the tremors that my body took that day. I will never forget. They make sure to teach you a lesson they think you need to learn," Merinda tells me.

"During my time, I got fucked by all of them, apart from Bryan and Cormack," Sue tells me, and before I can digest that bit, Jessica tells her she deserved it.

"Why?" I ask Jessica.

"Because Sue here knew very well Cormack had claimed her and went ahead and propositioned Bryan. Therefore, it was decided she should sample all of them to avoid such a scenario in the future."

"How about you?" I ask her.

"Meh. Just do everything in your power to avoid getting acquainted with Master Rio's whip."

"But Jessica, what exactly did you do to Arthur for him to let Rio whip you? Everyone knows Rio is a sadist," Merinda asked her, and I was curious to hear her answer.

"I was like Linnet here—green. Arthur had asked me what my fantasy was earlier, and I had jokingly told him that I wanted to have a threesome. So my rite was to have a threesome with Ben and your husband. I refused, and when Arthur insisted, I hit him in the balls."

"I'll do anything to avoid that whip. He gave me fifty lashes, and I had to count them out as he gave them and thank him," she says, and shudders.

I'm grateful because now I know how to avoid that whip under any circumstances.

I ask them why I am having the rite while I haven't agreed to this arrangement.

"I mean, he can't just marry me without my input, no way. When he told me earlier that I am his, I didn't take him seriously." I rise and head toward the room I left the men in.

Sue, who is heavily pregnant, blocks me and asks me to wait until Ben comes to pick me up and then to tell him about my reservations.

"I'm sorry you feel his way, Linnet, but those men out there—their word is the law. I would advise you to accept whatever they ask you to do. Their ideas seem high-handed, but they have good intentions.

"I have been with Arthur for the last six years, and I don't regret being his mate. Yes, I said mate, not wife. For a wife, you have the option of getting a divorce if it doesn't work out. With a mate, you work out your differences together. If it doesn't work, a brother arbitrates, but you'll be together.

"This condition makes one work on their relationship since there is no out. For whoever is in the wrong, the brotherhood offers punishment."

"Don't rush to pass judgment. We would love for you to join us. I can't wait 'til we are a full house, with every guy out there mated," Jessica tells me.

"How do you know it's Ben who'll come for me?" I ask out of curiosity

"For starters, Ben and Bryan are great friends. Then, he let Ben suck you off before he even did. It's not rocket science. Why don't we bet and see if I'm wrong?" Jessica asks excitedly.

The other two ladies look at her and decline. She pouts, and they laugh at her.

"I won't place a bet knowing I'll lose," Sue tells her.

"The last time I made a bet with you, I lost, and Briggs made sure I learned a lesson on why I should never bet if I'm not sure to win. So no thanks," Merinda pipes in.

"What did he do? Sometimes it gets hard to connect the public persona of our senator with your Dom," Sue tells her.

"He withheld my orgasms for a week. When he left on a trip, I made the mistake of using some toys. The bastard had a camera in our room, and to cut a long story short, I was introduced to Master Rio's whip."

"What? I never heard about that," Jessica demands, eyes wide and gleeful.

"That's because he was brought to our house, and…"

Before she finishes her sentence, Ben comes for me—just as Jessica predicted.

chapter FOURTEEN

BRYAN

To say I'm nervous is an understatement. I don't know how Linnet will react to all this.

All the preparations have been made. I want her to have a threesome, something I know she will enjoy.

I wait with bated breath, and Ben goes to get her from the ladies. Caleb, the tattooist, is already here, but I have to see her before I leave.

Once she comes with Ben, I know something is amiss, but before I can intervene, Arthur asks her about her impending divorce.

When she answers that she is ready to sign the papers, Arthur looks at me, and that's my cue to leave them alone.

I join Caleb in the next room, and he laughs at how tense I am. "Look, bro, take a deep breath; the sooner you relax, the sooner I get to work on you. Plus, you'll get back to your girl in time to watch her come on Ben's dick. Or maybe they'll have Rio give her a ride she will never forget."

"Not helping, Caleb," I tell him.

"Wasn't meant to. Now, lie on the table so I can work on you."

I force myself to calm down. Soon, the only sound in the room is the tattooing gun.

Linnet

Ben takes me to a dungeon-like room. All the guys, seven of them, are here. After listening to Jessica talk, I want to know who Master Rio is.

Master Arthur introduces all the guys in the room, and I realize I have met Ben already—popularly known as Master H.

Then there's Master Cormack, Master Sam, Master D—who is the senator—and finally, the infamous Master Rio.

Looking at him, you wouldn't think he'd harm a fly, but looks can be deceptive. Upon a closer look, he has cold eyes that seem to see through my bluff.

Master A asks if my husband is aware that I'm at the club. Once I assure him we have been separated for more than three years and I will get a divorce soon, he nods, and Bryan leaves the room.

I was tense before, but with Bryan gone, I am terrified.

Master A goes to the side table and fills his glass. My eyes follow him, and I don't see Master Rio approaching me.

When I catch him in my periphery, I take a step back. For every step I take, he takes one more, and soon, my back is to the wall. He stands in front of me and cages me in with his body. I feel trapped. It's delicious, but terrifying.

He lifts a hand and traces my face. "Relax, pet, I won't devour you now. But if you give me enough reasons, I will indulge you."

I take a deep breath that I didn't know I needed and look off to the side—anything to avoid that penetrating gaze.

"Lesson number one: you always look at your master when he is speaking to you, and right now, I happen to be your master. How does the thought of me being your master feel?"

"I..I…it's okay," I stammer my answer.

He grips my chin forcefully, and without intending it, a whimper leaves my lips.

"Lesson two: never lie to your master under any circumstances. So, will you indulge me with an answer, or should I get it from you?"

I close my eyes, take a deep breath. I wish I had the courage to slap this man's fresh ass out of my face. Who the hell does he think he is? I mean, he knows I'm terrified of him, and he wants to humiliate me further by demanding I answer him truthfully?

Then I remember Jessica telling me to avoid his whip. Taking a deep breath, I open my eyes and tell him he terrifies me.

"Good. Next time you hesitate to answer my questions, you won't like it. I don't like waiting for your answer. Next, I want you to go to the sink and wash off Bryan's come; I can smell it from here. I want that cunt clean before I take you."

I can't believe he just told me that I stink. I know I'm about to lose my cool. For heaven's sake, I am a grown-ass woman, not some toy to be kicked between these bastards. Who the hell do they think they are?

I take a step towards the door he indicated, and once I'm in the bathroom, I see that the window faces the balcony.

Something in me snaps. I'll teach these bastards a lesson they won't forget.

I have faced a lot in my life, but after everything is said and done, my dignity is all I have left. I'll look for alternative ways to raise the money I need for my daughter's surgery. I won't stoop so low and degrade myself like this; no man is worth it.

I stoke my anger as I climb through the window. The balcony opens to the kitchen, and I walk in as though I haven't a care in the world.

Sue sees me first and asks me if I ran away. I nod and start crying. I can't stand their pity, and I rise to leave.

Merinda tells me I'll need the code to all the doors.

"Sue, you can be our scapegoat. Give her your key, but here is my phone. Once you are out, give us a call so that we know you're safe."

"I can't take your phone," I tell her, but she tells me if I am serious, I should stop wasting time and take it. "It is your only way out. Once you reach the first floor, call for a cab. Use the staircase; that way, they can't stop you between the floors.

"Once out, let us know you're safe, and then switch the phone off. Call Jessica in two weeks," she tells me as she hands me a small backpack lifted from one of the cabinets.

What exactly am I evading? Have I just made my life situation even more dangerous? No time to panic now; I just need to get away. I hug them and leave; I don't know what will happen if I'm caught.

It takes me about fifteen minutes to leave the building. I haven't called for a cab yet; I was afraid someone would hear me and call the master.

At the gate, I pretend to be on a call and ignore the security guy, who's asking me if he should call a cab for me.

For once in my life, fate seems to be busy. A cab drops someone off, and I take it; once we're out of sight of the building, I call Jessica and assure them I'm fine.

I get home and pick up some essential documents and Chayla's clothes. It looks like I've just made everything worse, but the full consequences can descend on me later. I just have to make sure that my daughter and I are safe.

chapter FIFTEEN

I call Nina, and she tells me that she's at her mother's place. I ask her to meet me at her home, and if Bryan calls not to reveal my whereabouts.

"Then don't go to my place. It will be the first place he comes for you."

We decide I'll stay at a motel. She will visit me. I ask her to leave Chayla with her mother.

Times like now, I wish I had a car so that I could just drive off. I know I don't have a lot of money in my account, so I'll have to choose a cheap motel to stay at until I sort out my issues.

I then remember a quaint b&b Mike and I once stayed at, and I head there. Once I'm booked in, I take a shower and ask for their shepherd's pie and some hot chocolate. I want comfort food.

I sleep and am woken up by the ringing of the phone beside the bed. Nina came through, as always.

She lets me talk without interruption. "So let me get this straight—you ran from your wedding, or mating rites? Is this some kind of cult?"

I burst into tears right then and there. "I don't know!" I wail.

Nina sighs. "You know what, never mind. Okay, relax, think through everything. Then tomorrow, look for Mike. Let me finish; you broke your contract, so I don't think they will pay you. Chayla is not doing well, and since I thought you would have the money at the end of the week, I booked her surgery for next week. So swallow your pride, contact him, and get cash for my goddaughter's operation."

"I'm sorry I ran. I got scared," I tell her.

"It's high time, Linnet, that you learn to face your problems head-on. You've done a lot of running; it stops now. Bryan knew what you would face and asked you to trust him; you could have done it. Those ladies that assisted you in the running away, do you have an idea of what they will suffer for aiding you?

"Richie belongs to a club. I've never told you that since I didn't think you would understand. But now, you *are* in a position to understand. The pregnant lady may be off the hook, but you have just endangered the other two."

That fills me with terror. What exactly am I in for, then? But Nina talks before I can demand more information from her.

"Take care of Chayla, then go back and apologize properly. Take whatever is dished to you like a real woman. Because now that you've tasted the lifestyle, you won't be content until you're back. I love you, friend. You are the sister I never had, but you gotta do this right," she tells me, then leaves me to my thoughts.

chapter SIXTEEN

BRYAN

Once the tattoo is done, I take some time to gather my wits. I don't know what I'll find waiting for me. How has Linnet fared? I know I asked a lot from her when I told her to trust me blindly.

Trust is earned, and I am aware I haven't truly gained hers.

I take slow steps, but soon, I find myself in the room, but I see no Lynn.

Everyone is looking at me quite strangely. Both Jessica and Merinda are sporting reddened backsides. I know Rio's work when I see it: they are both tied up, and all the guys are drinking. Sue is sitting down, but I can see she's been crying.

I look at Arthur, and without waiting for my question, he tells me that with the help of the ladies, Linnet bolted.

"Rio asked her to wash her come off; she left via the window. Then these three aided her escape. Of course, Sue has taken all the blame. But we know they are in on it together. They thought since Sue can't be punished, they'll all escape.

"So since we can't find Merinda's phone, and she was sleeping in her room when all this was happening, we decided to let them tell us the truth. But even my mate won't admit to anything, so Rio decided to get some answers from them. But even after all the canes they've taken, they won't say anything," he tells me with a shrug. I can see how frustrated he is with the situation.

I know she will go to Nina's place, since that's where her kid is staying.

I ask Rio to get me Nina's number; he is a Secret Service agent who claims to hold a desk job. I know a field operative when I see one, and Rio has to be—even if he always denies it whenever we ask him.

After a few minutes, I have Nina's number. I call her, and she tells me she doesn't know where Lynn is—and yes, she has Chayla.

Rio's contacts let him know that Nina and her husband are members at a different club. I get his number and place a call to him. I will have Linnet's whereabouts before the day is over.

Jessica, who is a psychologist, asks to speak, and Arthur lets her. "Please—you guys have your code that you always tell us you can't break. We are simply following in your footsteps. Master A once told me that you would die for your brothers. We gained a sister today. You should let us also exercise our code and protect her."

"You think she needed protecting?" I ask her.

"She was scared, and we know once she has calmed down, she will realize she needs you."

"Let's hope so, sweetheart," Arthur tells her.

Richard, Nina's husband, calls me back with the address where Lynn is hiding. I decide to wait for her at the club. I tell him to let her know I'll wait for her until the end of the week.

I leave the room, head to bed, and sleep. I'm so tired, and there's nothing I can do tonight.

I decide to let Lynn go, for the time being. I'll give her a week, and if she isn't back by then, I'll wait.

I have her name inked on my back. Whether she will come willingly or not, I will have her in my life.

The week soon comes to an end, and Arthur gives me her check, which I decline. I'll take care of my woman, and I won't have her paid for spending time with me. No way.

"Look, I can have this mailed to her, but I want you to take it to her. Find out why she bolted. You guys had great chemistry. Jessica is a good judge of character, and if she helped her as a sister, it means there's a chance that she will be. But when you have her back, I want her here to give her my punishment."

I laugh at the way his eyes glint with that promise. I don't envy Linnet one bit. She will regret bolting for the rest of her life.

"What do you have planned for her?" I ask him, even though I know he won't tell me.

He is such a secretive bastard. In public, he's a federal judge, and I never want to face him in court.

Linnet

Barely two hours after Nina leaves, she calls me and tells me she's just sold me out.

I can't believe she'd just betray me like that, and I tell her so.

"Look, girlie, my Richie is very good with a cane. I don't want to be in a position where I can't lift my goddaughter. He promised to take good care of my hands. I've learned to pick my battles," she tells me unapologetically.

After this, I know I can't sleep here anymore. I decide to check the contents of the bag Merinda gave me.

It's like they knew I would bolt. The bag has a new burner phone with their numbers and a lot of money in it. At the bottom of the bag, there is a note saying I should use the cash to get my daughter the medical attention she deserves.

I cry as I realize what these ladies have done for me. It's late, and they're probably in their suites with their husbands. But they are expecting my call, so I place one to Sue. The chances of her getting in trouble are minimal.

She answers on the first ring. "Took you long enough to call."

"How is everything back there?" I ask her.

"Just like we expected. Both Jessica and Merinda look great with red backsides."

"God. If I knew that was coming, I wouldn't have involved you guys."

She tells me that we ladies have to stand and fight our battles together. But she discloses that I will take her punishment when I get back.

"What if I don't come back?" I ask her with a dark smirk. She's so sure that I'll go back.

"Can you imagine a life without your Master? Don't answer me; think about it and make up your mind. But after what you subjected Jess and Mer to, you should name your second and third kids after them," she tells me, then cuts the connection.

This is all so insane—but now I have the money for Chayla's surgery, or at least most of it. Things are going to be okay.

I could walk away right now.

So why am I hesitating? Have I completely lost my mind?

I may not have Bryan's name tattooed on my back, but I can't imagine a life without him. He has changed my way of thinking—its time I do what makes me happy. Nina is right, I always avoid anything that will pull me away from my comfort zone.

Bryan, pushes all my limits. I know I already trust him with my body, but it's time I did the same with my heart—trust that he will keep his promise, to care for me. Maybe this time karma will let me get what I want.

I know I don't deserve him, but I will do anything to make him proud of me. I'll show the world that I'm not ashamed to be by his side. Now that I know my girl is going to be alright, it is time I take care of the man I have fallen for, the man who has shown me how to love again.

chapter SEVENTEEN

I spent the night and decided what I wanted to do. I call Nina and tell her I'll pick Chayla up in the morning and take her to the hospital.

Once at the hospital, things fall back into perspective. My daughter's health takes the highest priority, and once she is booked for surgery, I decide to visit Mama.

I call ahead and tell her I would like to meet with her.

"Lynn, my dear girl, you know this is your home, and you don't need to book an appointment with me—even though I have a bone to pick with you," she tells me.

I swallow. At least she's not angry with me. She has every right to be, considering. But I get a ride out anyway.

The Payne mansion always takes my breath away. With its privacy fence and its massive front door, it always made me feel like I was entering a palace.

I ring the bell, and Catrina, their long-time housekeeper, opens it. When she finds it's me, she hugs me; she always made me feel like a young girl.

"I never dreamt this would be possible, that I would get to hold my girl again. How have you been? Don't answer that; I can see you've not been taking care of yourself. I told you a woman with a great figure like yours should ensure it stays nice and full. Do you want to be all skin and bones? Now, I have a few recipes that you are just going to love."

She drags me to the kitchen. I always loved Catrina and her chatter. And I always loved her home-style, authentic northern Mexican cooking just as much.

"Stop monopolizing my girl," Mama tells her from the kitchen, where she is making ginger cookies as always. Despite being filthy rich, Mama Payne still bakes the goodies that she takes to the various children's homes.

My time here was always spent in the kitchen between these two. Mama hugs me, and I find myself crying.

I have wronged this woman, who's been like a second mother to me. At the time, I was afraid and thought I could do things my own way, and on my own, but now I regret what I did.

Once we are seated with glasses of milk and ginger cookies, I try to come up with what to tell them.

"Just spit it out. I can see you are dying to tell us something," Mama tells me, taking a sip of chocolate milk. If she could have chocolate with everything, she says, she would be happy.

"Finish up your milk first; I don't want you to pour it on me once you hear what I have to tell you."

"There's nothing you can tell me that's worse than when you walked out of my son's life without a backward glance. You know, I waited for you to come here so that we could talk. I never gave up, and now you're here. Better late than never, but you might be too late. We waited a long time."

God, how am I going to tell her that she has a three-year-old granddaughter whom I haven't introduced to her?

I regret it so much that soon, I'm crying. It was selfish of me to keep Chayla from these two wonderful women. But what's done is done; I'll have to come clean, and damn the consequences.

So I rise, and facing the windows, I watch her gardens as I tell her about my girl. At first, she is quiet; I don't want to turn back and watch the betrayal I know I'll see on her face.

"What have I ever done that made you think that you couldn't trust me? Lynn, when Mike introduced you to me, I took you in like my daughter, and not as Mike's wife. If you and Mike couldn't solve your issues, I wanted to still have my girl with me. Was it wrong for me to think that? Answer me this; what did he do that made you run away while expecting?"

"She what?" Mike bellows as he comes into the kitchen.

I never heard him come in, and now my worst nightmare is coming to life.

"Linnet, can you tell me exactly what happened? And you, Mike, you keep quiet. Every time I asked you what happened, you never answered me," she tells Mike.

"It's not important, Mama! I made a mistake by not introducing you to your granddaughter, and that's why I came," I say.

"Come on, don't play the victim card. If you wanted the family to meet this so-called daughter of yours, you could have done it ages ago," a lady I haven't seen before scornfully retorts, before I can say a word.

"Darling, please, not now," Mike tells her.

"She's a gold digger; she wants to get money from you," she says while opening the fridge to get some juice.

I find it odd that neither Mama nor Catrina offers her anything.

"Lynn, why? I know I messed up, but I loved you. Despite everything I did, didn't I deserve the right to know my daughter?" he asks brokenly.

I look back at the gardens. I'm so terrified and anxious, I'm light-headed, but this is it. The moment of truth. "That day, I came home earlier. I was coming from the doctor's. But you were otherwise occupied."

"What did you do to drive her away?" Mama won't let it go, and I wait to hear what he tells her.

"I betrayed her trust."

"With her?" Mama asks him. "Michael Dickson Payne, you will answer me," she tells him as she rises from her chair. Mama is a force to reckon with, and she rarely gets mad, but when she does, nobody can stop her.

She whacks his back. I can tell she'd give him an old-fashioned smack or two, but I have to pipe in.

"Mama, please, there's something I haven't told you yet." I can see the relief on Mike's face. "Chayla is sick, and she will be undergoing surgery in two days."

The silence that follows is absolute; Mama takes her seat and looks at me.

"I told you she needs money; chances are, she's lying to get money from your family," Mike's girlfriend tells him.

"Becky, you open that filthy mouth of yours again, and I will clean it with soap," Catrina tells her. I have never heard so much venom coming from her mouth. She was always this motherly figure who helped Mama raise her three kids.

"I don't take orders from the paid help," Becky retorts.

Wasn't Mike supposed to have some girlfriend he was seeing? So much for that, I think to myself, dismayed. And it doesn't seem like this girl is an upgrade.

Mike orders her to keep quiet or leave. She opts for silence.

"So, Lynn, tell us exactly what happened once you left my despicable son."

I take a deep breath. "I went to stay at my friend's place but later moved to a hostel once she reconciled with her husband. I had a difficult pregnancy, and between classes, jobs, and hospitals, I was worn out.

"When I went into labor, I was fragile, and my chances of survival were low. I called Mike, but his secretary stonewalled me. I gave the hospital your number as my next of kin, in case I didn't make it. My calls were never answered here.

"Chayla was underweight and had to stay at the hospital for a few weeks. Nina called Mike, and he didn't want to hear anything concerning me. So once I got discharged, I went my own way with my baby girl." I feel worn out reliving the past.

"What's wrong with my granddaughter?"

I tell them about Chayla's heart condition, and by the time I'm done, Mama is on her way out. She doesn't even know which hospital my girl was admitted to.

She calls for her driver and demands that her husband, Mike Senior, come along. I miss him. Michael Senior—or Big Mike—is a bear of a man, and a good man at that. "We are going to the hospital to meet your granddaughter," Mama tells him on her way out.

He comes over, hugs me, and asks how she is.

"Wait a minute, did you know about this?" Mama asks him.

"Bryan called a while back, letting me know I couldn't borrow his plane. When I told him I wanted to take it to the South Coast, he explained why he needed it. He wants her to have the surgery at his hospital, with the best cardiologists and equipment."

I clasp my hands over my mouth.

Of course. Bryan's a doctor. And he's just pulled strings to make sure that my daughter will get her surgery. But how am I going to afford *this*?

chapter EIGHTEEN

BRYAN

Once I leave the club, I head to my penthouse. Looking around, I know it's not a conducive environment for raising a family.

I call Sam. He owns real estate and sometimes does work for my firm. He'll know if there's a place suitable for a family that I can buy outright. Next, I call Richard, who tells me that Chayla is due for an operation in two days and gives the hospital where it will take place.

I call the doctors in charge of Chayla's care and request a transfer. I ask to join as her doctor and perform the operation at our hospital. The next call is to Dad; I need the family's jet to transfer her.

Lynn doesn't pick up my call, but when Dad tells me she's at home with Mama, I relax. At least I know she isn't ignoring my calls.

As soon as I met Chayla earlier, I fell in love with her. She's small for her age but a brave little girl. "Ankle Brwen!" she calls at me now.

"Yes, princess?" I hug her as I look at Nina.

She shrugs as though it's not a big deal that my niece knows me. Once she's busy with her dolls, she asks when her mama will join her.

"She pwomised to be with me when they make me better," she says, sucking her thumb.

"Mama is coming with your Nana and Papa," I tell her.

"And Daddy? Mama told me Daddy would come to see me get bettew,"

Nina calls Lynn, then gives the phone to Chayla. As I watch her chat with her mama, I know that this is it for me. All I want is to protect and cherish this little angel.

Dad calls to ask me where we are; I give him the room number in the private wing. I know they're on their way here, but I can't stand still. I want to see Lynn, and before I know what I'm doing, I leave the room and catch them as they round the corner.

I walk towards them, and once Lynn sees me, she just sprints.

It takes a second to decide I don't care what they will say as I open my arms wide.

My initial intention is to hug her, but once she's in my arms, I can't help myself. I dip my head and capture her lips. The kiss starts innocently but soon gets hot.

If it wasn't for Mama whacking me in the head with her bag, I could have carried on. I look at Lynn's eyes and see the moment she realizes what we have just done — kissed like teenagers in front of my parents and her husband.

I see guilt there, and before she can say anything and dig a grave wide enough for both of us, I tell them that Chayla wants her. She leaves me with my family and rushes to her daughter's side.

"Son, I know this is not the time, but we need to talk," Dad tells me as he takes Mama's hand and follows Lynn.

"How long have you been screwing my wife? That goody-two-shoes left me because of some indiscretion, and yet here she is, shacking up with you?"

"You know something, Mike? I'll forget you're my brother if you speak ill of Lynn again. Got it?"

"Forget like you did when you started with her? Tell me something. Have you tainted her with your club?"

Red swims in front of my eyes. I speak in a growl. "Mike, don't push me..."

"Or what? You going to hit me?"

"Go visit your daughter. She's been asking about you," I tell him.

"Is she even mine? She says I betrayed her, but this hurts, brother. I thought blood was thicker than water, but it means shit to you."

I know he is hurt and feels betrayed. But I would never intentionally set out to hurt him. We will have some words; I hope it doesn't break us, because Linnet is it for me. If I have to choose, Mike can sit and stew. He had years to pursue Linnet—this is just sour grapes.

Linnet

I rush into the hospital room and hug my daughter.

"What happened?" Nina asks me

"Fuck! I just messed up big."

"Mama, you said a bad word," Chayla tells me as she snuggles into my chest.

"What did you do?" Nina asks me urgently. I tell her I'll fill her in on it later. Right then, Mama and Dad come in, and all talk ceases. They are busy doting on their granddaughter.

"What's your name, angel?" Papa asks her.

"Chayla Bookes Payne," she answers proudly.

Mama looks at me, and I can see tears glinting in her eyes.

"I know you are Papa, Nana, and that's my daddy," she says as she points at Mike, who is standing at the door.

She raises her arms so that Mike can pick her up. When she's not in pain, she is a feisty little girl, and I know she will have them eating out of her hands soon.

Mike picks her up and looks at me over her head. I don't think he'll ever forgive me for denying him so much time with his daughter. He looks incredibly wounded.

But I stare back at him. He didn't pick up my calls. He cheated on me. He dug this grave himself. Never test a single mother; you'll break first.

He finally quails and looks back at Chayla.

Bryan joins us, and the tension in the room is so thick you can cut it with a knife.

Chayla tires quickly, and once she does, I lay her down and go to the doctor's office to get an update. Nina follows me and waits outside the door.

Once I'm done, she demands to know why the room was so tense. So I tell her what happened.

Nina sits back, taking it all in. "Goddamn. Admit it and deal with the consequences, girlie. Let me ask—when Mike came back, did you hug him, let alone kiss him? But with Bryan, you forget yourself. That's what is crazy."

I know what I want, and where I belong—but it would be an absolutely insane decision.

But at least my baby girl's taken care of. Now I just have to clean up my own mess.

Oh, god. I have no idea what I'm ever going to do.

chapter NINETEEN

The operation is successful, and my daughter is on the road to recovery. I've been staying at the hospital as often as possible for the last three weeks while my daughter was in intensive care. She is being released, and Bryan takes care of the discharge papers.

I don't ask him about the bills, since he has been so professional throughout, but I know that at some point, we'll have to address the issue between us.

I miss the closeness we had developed at the club. I don't know what he's thinking after I bailed out, but if he will give another chance, I'll show him I trust him with everything that I have. I will never run away from my fears again.

I expect he'll have his driver take me and Chayla to our old place, but I soon find we're heading in the opposite direction.

We arrive at a gated community. Whenever I imagined his home, I always pictured him living in a penthouse.

It's a beautiful place, with lots of space and a pool at the back. He gives me a tour of the home, and the only room I really notice is the kitchen.

"Whose place is this?" I ask him, dreading the answer.

"Ours," he tells me. "I had your things moved over. They are in the garage. You will unpack at your convenience."

"What about your place?"

"I rented it out, and my things are also in the garage. We'll pick what will fit here; the rest, we can donate to Goodwill."

"You moved me out of my place without my consent?" I ask him, gobsmacked and sure he's lost his mind. *Does he really think he can just order me around—to this extent?*

"It wasn't needed, since either way, you were moving in with me."

"I'm your brother's wife, for heaven's sake!" I feel like smacking his white ass.

"Not anymore. I got you both divorced."

"I didn't sign any paperwork. I'll have to call Mike."

He lets me call Mike, and I'm surprised to hear that he received signed divorce papers from me. Mike asks to meet when I have time, since he wants to discuss everything in person.

"You know, you're impossible. Which judge approved the divorce without our signatures?"

"I took advantage of the connections I have. Besides, you actually signed the papers."

He shows me the papers—which were tacked on together with Chayla's medical paperwork.

I'm both happy and furious. I try to put my anger and disbelief into words. "You took advantage of my absentmindedness. I trusted you when you gave me those papers."

Though I'm delighted to be finally divorced from Mike, I don't like the way Bryan did it. He doesn't seem to understand that I am an adult, capable of making my own decisions.

At my protestations, he just looks self-satisfied. "You should read every paper before you sign it. I wish you had shown the same blind trust when I asked you to," he tells me.

BRYAN

I know I'm demanding, but if I let Lynn have her way, she would never let me back in her life. Taking advantage of her vulnerable state wasn't my brightest or most ethical idea, but the end justifies the means.

My brother is a proud man, but I knew once he received the paperwork, he would sign.

I ensured Lynn got custody of Chayla, though Mike is getting unlimited access to her. Lynn won't have a problem with that—it was her own freedom that concerned her.

Once they've settled in, I have to meet with Dad. I promised him that once Chayla was out of the hospital, I would visit him, and I have to keep my word.

When I get home, I find Dad in the study.

"Why, of all the women in the world, did you have to go for your brother's wife?"

"When I met her, she was wearing a mask, and by the time I realized who she was, it was too late. I love her, Dad."

"When was this?"

"I met Lynn a month ago, but they've been apart for years. I know Mike has moved on, so I didn't hesitate to take her."

"Have you claimed her yet?"

To say I am shocked is an understatement. How does Dad know about my proclivities?

"You think I stay in here, watching life pass me by? I know about your club. So answer me."

"I was about to when she bolted."

"And now you won't give her the same opportunity. I know you bought a house on the other side of town."

It seems Dad is aware of everything I have been up to. "Talk with your brother; explain exactly how you met Lynn. He's a reasonable lad; he will understand you, though perhaps not immediately."

Mama offers me a smile as I leave and some cookies to take to Lynn. How did she know Lynn is with me? At least she's not treating me coldly or interrogating me.

I leave before she can ask what is troubling me. How do they know Lynn and I are together?

I let it pass as I head home. All the way, I think about how to approach my brother.

But I'm surprised when I find his car parked outside our house. He can come and visit Chayla, but I would rather he did it when I was aware of his impending visit.

LINNET

Once Bryan leaves, Mike calls me and asks if he can come over. Despite my irritation at Bryan, I'm relieved to have this done. It'll feel good to get the conversation over with, and I tell him it's okay.

"I realized you didn't ask for anything from me, and this place is an expensive one. How will you maintain the place? Did Dad buy it for you?"

"No, it's Bryan's," I tell him.

"When did you meet Bryan?"

I lie terribly, so I don't bother lying. I tell him the truth.

His jaw drops. "You? At a sex club?"

"Yes. Things change. You try a few things to see what works and what doesn't."

I can't tell him why I was there in the first place. I don't correct his misinterpretation. Better he thinks I went there seeking an adventure.

The topic soon changes to our daughter. He wants to know how Chayla's doing, how things have been with her. I've taken videos of Chayla as she grew up, and I let him watch them. I have documented every milestone in her life.

That, of course, just leads to more questions—as I should have expected. "Why, Lynn? Help me understand. Was your pride more important than the welfare of our child? God, do you know how I felt when you spoke of a difficult pregnancy?" Mike asks me. He doesn't give me a chance to answer; he just stands up and comes to where I am seated and kneels.

Taking my face, he wipes away the tears that I didn't know were falling from my eyes.

"All I ever wanted in life was to treat you like the princess you are. For heaven's sake, I took away your virginity, and you made me promise you never to hurt you. Yes, it was wrong that I betrayed your trust, but how did you end up in a sex club? Bryan calls it a gentlemen's club, but you and I know very well—there are no 'gentlemen' there."

I ended up telling him how I came to know about the club and how I met Bryan.

Mike tells me he's grateful that I met his brother—though he shudders when he thinks what would have happened if I met Rio instead.

I'm surprised that he knows Rio. "Those guys are Bryan's friends. He calls them his brothers. I've accompanied him to the club several times since you left, so I know how it is."

"Are you a member?" I ask him

"And pay that huge registration fee? I'd rather head to Vegas and try my luck there," he says with a laugh.

Somehow, I can't picture Mike at the club.

We talk about our failed marriage, and I begin to understand that he never meant to hurt me. He was trying to protect me from what he thought was something I couldn't handle.

We agree to let him visit as often as possible and, once Chayla is well, to let him bring her to his mother's place.

I look at Mike, and for a moment, I regret everything I've done. I hope we'll get another chance at being friends. What we have is a little bit unorthodox—I don't know how the world will view our relationship.

We hug. When he's about to leave, Bryan walks in. I tense because I don't know what he will think.

"Relax. Don't show him you're afraid of him. After all, we're not doing anything wrong," Mike whispers in my ear.

Slowly I exhale a breath I didn't know I was holding and turn towards Bryan.

God, I love him; I didn't mean to fall for him. But I would be lying if I said I didn't love him...

"You're back," I chirp, trying to diffuse the tension that has already risen in the room.

"Yes, I am," he tells me, then asks to have a chat with Mike in the study.

chapter TWENTY

BRYAN

I dread having this chat with my brother, but I have to.

Once in the study, I head towards the cabinet and get him his scotch while I fill a glass with my favorite whiskey.

I have never been a coward, and knowing I let Mike down is weighing on me.

I gulp down the contents of my whiskey, and the little shit laughs. "God, I never thought I'd live to see you this nervous. It's a good look," he tells me with a cocky grin.

I don't get it. How can he be this calm? I expected at least a left hook, if nothing else.

"Though I'm enjoying myself immensely at your misery, Mama brought me up better. Lynn filled me in on what happened at the club. Man, how I wish I was there to see your reaction the moment you realized you had just fucked your brother's wife."

"It wasn't my best moment, I assure you. So, Lynn told you what happened, and you just believed her?"

"I knew Lynn for three years before we started dating. We dated for two years and were married for three years. And in all that time, she's never given me a reason to doubt her. I don't think she'll start now," he tells me, taking a look around my new study.

I envy him the time he's had with Lynn, but we'll have our own time together. Mike mostly kept her away from the family; intensely private and secretive, he and Lynn had eloped. Of course, I've been focused on my own career until now, so I barely cared. Let Mike do what he likes—I won't make the same mistake. She will have the life she deserves with me.

This time, she will have a real relationship ahead of her, a real family.

I tell Mike my side of the story, and I'm glad we had this talk. Once he is gone, I'll have to make Lynn officially mine.

She doesn't know it yet, but tomorrow, we'll get married. I have organized a civil wedding.

I know Arthur is organizing the mating ritual. I asked for some time so that we could take care of Chayla's treatment. But now, that angel is on her way to completely healing.

Thinking about her brings a smile to my face. Her cardiologist advised us to let her take it easy until she makes a full recovery. She is in her room, and even her nurse is allowed in—though only after she is appropriately attired as a princess.

Chayla's full of life, playing until she's almost falling off her feet with tiredness. I know I'm spoiling her, but she's my princess.

Her room has all the things that a princess would possibly require. She loves the Barbie dolls Nina helped me pick. But the icing on the cake is the castle; I have to agree, I went overboard with that one—but I'll never admit it to Lynn.

I tell Mike about the castle, and he tells me next time I'm going shopping for her, I should call him.

"Chayla has been through hell; we'll give her a slice of heaven, bro. Lynn will join us when she realizes we're not backing down."

"But I don't want her to be one of those spoiled rich kids. I want her to grow up knowing the value of what she has, not having everything she desires handed over like that," Lynn tells us from the doorway.

I never heard her coming, but I'm thankful for her. I know between her and Mama, we won't spoil Chayla too much. They'll never allow us to get away with it. I smile at her warmly. "Of course. But we'll balance it all out."

Lynn snorts but allows a small smile. "Come on, guys; dinner is ready."

We head down to the kitchen, where we find Chayla already throwing a tantrum. She's on a special diet, but she wants to eat what we're having.

LINNET

Once the Payne brothers head towards the study, I get busy in the kitchen. I love cooking, and with a well-equipped kitchen like this, I'm in heaven.

I open the cabinets and the fridge and find them both well-stocked. I consider cooking some chicken, but then I feel adventurous. Why not lasagna?

I gather all the ingredients, knowing that I'll have to prepare two separate meals: one for us and the other one for Chayla. It will have to look identical to what we're having, so she won't be the wiser.

Balancing what she's supposed to eat and what she wants to eat has been an uphill battle. But the latest test results have shown marked improvements.

Still, with Chayla sorted, I have other things to worry about.

Tomorrow, I'll have to visit Mama and clear the air; I don't know whether she will have any issues with this relationship I have with Bryan.

After Mike leaves, I tell Bryan of my impending visit to his mother.

"Mama will give you a hard time, but she loves you too much to stay angry. She'll be on your side. But we've got an errand to run before you visit Mama. Call her and tell her you'll pass by her place in the afternoon."

After the way I let him down before, I agree with what he wants, hoping to redeem myself.

But one thing I'm sure of is that I'm not ready for this mating ceremony—this ritual. I wish Nina were on my side, but as it is, she's so judgmental. I know what I did was cowardly, but I deserve some understanding.

Honestly, I feel betrayed. One day, I'll tell her what she's put me through. I always thought she would be someone I could count on, but this time, she's let me down.

After I do the cleanup and check on my baby girl, I head to the master bedroom.

I wish I could head into one of the guestrooms, curl up on the bed, and think about my life. I love having everything set up in an orderly manner, but right now, I'm living in utter chaos. I'm in way over my head.

On my way to the master bedroom, I find the study's light still on. Bryan is seated on the couch, nursing a beer.

"Well…well, I never thought to see you with a beer. Thought whiskey was your poison," I tell him as I take the opposite seat.

"Shows how much you know about me and my tastes," he tells me with a shrug.

I feel so bad for running away from the ceremony.

I rise from my seat and take a step towards him, hoping that he doesn't send me away.

He pats his lap, indicating he wants me to sit there. I take it as an olive branch and tentatively move closer to him.

He grabs my hand, and I squeal as I land across his thighs. I can feel the heat of his body, and my nipples pebble immediately. I'm not wearing a bra, and I know he can see them hardening.

He holds my chin and raises it so I can't hide from him.

"I told you to never hide from me. Why are you hiding your beautiful face from me?"

I take a breath, exhale, and hope that was a rhetorical question, but when I look into his eyes, I know he expects an answer.

I hate how exposed and vulnerable I feel. And yet, something about that rawness makes me crave it, too. It's just so compelling, this tension of desire and frustration.

If I lie to him, I might get a spanking, which I don't want. Jessica told me that this would be forever—and in case of differences, we'll have to work them out. Last time things went wrong, I just left. That's what I do.

It's not an option this time, and I'm oddly grateful.

But I'm still afraid of what will happen if it doesn't work. What if he falls in love with someone else? I can't go through another rejection. And what would it do to Chayla?

Well, as Nina told me, it's time I take control of my destiny.

"I am afraid—afraid of what will happen if this doesn't work out. Afraid I won't be enough for you, of not meeting your expectations. I've already failed you once; I don't want to do that again. But I know I'm not ready for the mating ceremony. I don't think I'll ever be ready for it."

"It's okay to be nervous, and I'm worried, as well. But it's something that has to be done. The sooner we do it, the better for us. I want to settle down with you and watch my mate blossom with my baby. To have that, we have to have the ceremony behind us. Take this consolation; you've got great friends who want you to succeed." He smiles tenderly. "I can just imagine how excited Nina and even Jessica will be."

I hope he's right, and I hope it's enough.

chapter TWENTY ONE

The following day, we wake up late. I thought Bryan would have left for work, but I'm surprised to find him in Chayla's room, dressing her dolls. If he doesn't watch it, she'll have him wrapped around her tiny finger.

I ask if they've had their breakfast and am surprised that he managed to get her to drink some milk.

He asks me to go to the guest room and pick up my gift, and once I'm done, wait for him there.

It feels like ages since he gave me orders, and this makes me very happy. I don't take time to analyze it; I just know that I want to please him.

In the guestroom, I find a dress that is so beautiful, I'm afraid to put it on. The dress accentuates all my curves, making me feel statuesque.

I know I am pretty, but this dress is a showstopper. It fits me like a second skin, meaning I can't have any panties or the lines will show. If I didn't know better, I would have thought it was a wedding dress. With its off-white color, I can imagine getting married in this. The contrast of cream against my dark, rich skin tone is stark and stunning. I'm sure I look like an angel.

But I know our marriage will be at the club—with me naked, probably on my knees, giving a blowjob to some guy I don't know.

That does sound fun, but it also makes my heart sink. My reality now seems so far removed from what my life was like a month ago. Every time I think of what will happen in that club, I get goosebumps. This time, I'll go in with my eyes open—but it means I can't run away claiming ignorance.

But if the last couple of weeks have taught me anything, it's the dedication Bryan has to my girl and me.

As I dress, I vow never to let him down again. I'll do whatever the club expects me to do and spend the rest of my life obeying him. But I know it will be an uphill struggle.

I love taking his orders, just like now. I didn't know how much I missed it until I heard his voice take that note that says I'd better do what he asks or face the consequences.

Once I'm dressed, I look in the closet mirror to see how it fits once again—and that's when I see him leaning against the door.

For such a huge guy, he sure walks stealthily. I never hear him move. I watch him watch me in the mirror.

My breath hitches. I can tell he's up to something. He's got that twinkle in his eye that he always has whenever he wants to do something that I won't like.

I watch him walk towards me, and my senses tingle. I am taking a deep breath. I stand still as he reaches me.

He hugs me tightly from behind. I can feel how hard he is, and as he starts playing with my nipples, I surrender. I lean into him so that he can support my weight.

"You know you look ravishing, but something is missing, my angel."

I try to turn. I know this dress needs a necklace, but I thought my pearls would do. It sweeps down to reveal the perfect amount of collarbone and cleavage, and the blank space demands something. But Bryan doesn't allow me to turn. He takes me with him and lays me down, and I try to rise, so as not to crease the dress.

"You either lie still, or I'll rip it off—your choice," he tells me with a hard glint in his eyes. Damn it. Whenever he uses this tone of voice, I just melt. I have come to know most of his tells, and I know how to pick my battles.

I try squeezing my thighs discreetly together to alleviate my arousal and get some relief without him getting wise.

But he's got my number; there's no winning with him. "Spread those legs; I want to have a taste before we leave."

He raises his amazing, deep-blue eyes. Every time I gaze into them, I get lost.

He raises my dress, and I'm aware again of how the off-white color of the dress contrasts starkly with my dark skin.

He takes a deep breath, inhaling me, and my arousal warms every inch of my body. It's hard to understand how a guy like this could want me in his life, but here I am. And he's intoxicated merely by my scent, stroking my legs ever so gently and massaging my inner thighs.

"Good girl. It seems you've learned how to take my orders. Thought you had forgotten," he tells me appreciatively, realizing I'm not closing my legs.

I try to regulate my breath. I know he will let me come when he wants, and no amount of begging will quicken it.

He then dips his fingers between my lips, and I know he can feel how wet I am. I can feel the little trickle of desire rising from deep within me. I know once I start, I won't stop.

He presses on my clit, and I can feel sparks behind my eyelids.

I unconsciously squirm, and he holds me down.

God, it's been almost a month since he last touched me; last night, while he slept, I went into the bathroom and made myself come. But it never quenched my desire. I slept fitfully, hoping that he would put me out of my misery.

I pray that he won't find out—I can't bear his punishment right now. He told me that he controls my orgasms and that I'll come only with his approval.

I tried, but it was too much. Sleeping in Bryan's arms was a torture. I thought he would make love to me, but he just held me and promptly fell asleep. I never thought I would experience sexual frustration with him in my life, and yet, here we are.

"And you love this," he tells me as he inserts three fingers at the same time. I'm not prepared for the barrage of emotions and sensations. "Ohhhh...ahhh!" I cry, about to detonate.

I can feel his heavy gaze on me as he plays with my folds. I'm at the brink of going off the edge, but I know I have to wait for his go-ahead.

He runs his thumb along my clit, which shoots tendrils of pleasure through my body, then pumps his fingers in me twice. He stops and removes them.

"So that you know, I'll finger-fuck you, but you won't come. Do you have anything to say regarding last night?"

How did he know? I mean, I never made a noise, and he was sound asleep when I left him.

I tense as his fingers hit against my g-spot. He holds still and looks at me expectantly. I want him to massage me there, but I know until I come clean, he won't give me the sheer ecstasy that I'm longing for right now.

"You love it too much; that's not acceptable for you right now. You will come as your punishment, not as a reward." He looks expectantly at me, but at least his fingers are still buried deep within me.

"I am sorry, Sir. It will never happen again," I apologize in the hope that he won't leave me with unfulfilled desires.

He just looks at me as though he expects more.

"I was so horny last night. I didn't mean to, but once I was in the bathroom, I lost control."

"Were your fingers better than my cock?"

"No, Sir."

"Have I made you afraid to approach me whenever you have an issue?" he asks me as he presses on my clit. "If you come without my authorization, I'll have your ass so hot and red, you won't sit down for the whole of next week."

Looking at how determined he is, I shake my head.

He then removes his fingers from my pussy and places them at my mouth. Opening up, I clean his fingers and watch his eyes, and the smoldering desire there turns me on even more.

He watches me clean his fingers, then asks me how I taste. But before I can answer, he turns to the bedside drawer and tells me he is going to reward me for my behavior last night.

I would give an arm to know what he considers a fitting gift for my behavior.

He retrieves two pink objects and asks me if I know what they are.

Once I tell him I don't, he edges closer to me and kneels beside the bed.

That's when I get a closer view of the objects; they are clamps designed like tiny earrings.

My experience with clamps is still vivid in my mind. And as he clips my left pussy lip, the clamp is firm, but not painful. Once done, he clamps my right pussy lip, and I know there's nothing like a reward here.

The clamps are designed in a way that they rest on my clit, and I know that once I stand, the gravity will take care of my downfall.

He then gives me his hand and helps me stand. The clamps rest on my clit. My entire body seizes with the bombardment of sensations.

"How does it feel?" he asks.

"I don't know. It's not comfortable, and at the same time, it is," I answer honestly.

He tells me to ensure my legs have some give when walking, and also while sitting. "Every time you think of your orgasm, remember, I'll always control them. This is the latest design, which is meant for long-term use. Do not at any time remove them. I put them there, and I will remove them."

That makes me shudder with desire and longing. He won't let me come without his permission, and the refusal is intoxicating.

He then leads me to the car. I love the way he puts his arm at my back. It makes me feel cherished and loved.

Chapter TWENTY TWO

When we arrive in downtown Austin, we head to the courthouse. I'm surprised—I wasn't expecting to be brought here.

When I turn to ask him what we're doing here, he just looks at me with an expression that speaks volumes. I follow him without asking the questions that press at me like the clips.

We get to the civil registry, and somehow, I'm not surprised to find Nina and Ben.

To say that I am pissed is an understatement. Why does Bryan think I'll marry him when he hasn't even proposed?

Nina just shakes her head, and at that moment, I hate her so much, I wish I could wring her neck. She just forgot the girls' code and betrayed me. Again.

"Do I have a choice?" I whisper to Bryan, who has his eyes fixed elsewhere—so much that I can't tell whether he's trying to avoid my gaze or he's genuinely interested in something.

I shoot him a glare. If looks could kill, he would be dead by now.

He ignores my question. I know only a few hours have passed since I vowed to submit to him, but this is very high-handed of him.

Taking a deep breath, I repeat the vows, sign the documents, and leave. They have to know I did this under duress.

When Nina reaches me, she asks me to stop behaving like a brat. For once in my life, I give her the finger. I expect her to be shocked, but she just laughs.

"See ya tonight. Hope you will be in a better mood—for your sake, I might add. Act spoiled, and expect treatment in kind, girlfriend."

I never knew that I could hate her this much. Payback is a bitch. I'll get her one of these days.

When he joins me in the car, I expect him to tell me how disappointed he is. But he just drives off, and soon, we are turning into his parents' compound.

Bryan

I know Lynn is pissed off, but if I don't nip this in the bud right now, she'll never learn to trust me in everything. Left to her own devices, we would have married on our deathbeds, or just before then, and no sooner.

Looking at her as I drive towards my parents' home, I know she's seething, but she is learning to curb her anger.

If she behaves, I might reward her for good behavior.

I drop her at the gate and tell her I'll pick her up at five o'clock. This, I know, will give her ample time to vent and cool off.

Tonight, we're having the ceremony, and this time, she will see it through. If I have to tie her down for it, then I shall.

I know she needs to learn how to control her instinct to run away. I'll always be there for her, and unlike Mike, I won't abandon her.

Talking with Arthur the other day drove home what I didn't want to admit: Lynn is a runner, and she's very insecure in everything she does. It's time I step up and bring her walls down. Show her that she has nothing to fear, and her past doesn't define who she is. Yes, she had to leave, and yes, she's used to people leaving. I understand that she wants to run before people can leave her—but I'm not going anywhere, not without her.

It's going to be an uphill battle, but I'm ready to climb it.

I call Ben, and together, we head to the club, where we find the rest of my brothers waiting.

"I thought you'd bring her a bit earlier," Rio tells me, but I know he's joking.

I don't know what the bastard has planned, but I'm sure he's up to something. And knowing Lynn left while in his care, he'll teach her a lesson she won't be forgetting any time soon.

"I don't envy you, your comfort today. At least being out of the room keeps your sanity intact and your imagination active," Commack tells me as he joins Ben and me at the bar.

"Don't…"

"Okay, but watching you sweat will be the highlight tonight. And a little birdie told me that since your mate runs, she'll be participating in the rituals for longer than usual."

Things are somehow better than I expected, considering this is the first time someone's mate ran away from the ceremony. I know it reflects poorly on my mastery techniques.

But I don't think I can punish Linnet for bailing. She's new to this, and if I'm honest with myself, I rushed her.

I am disappointed in myself for what my ill-preparedness is going to cost her, but I know I'll spend the rest of our lives making it up to her.

In my mind, I keep seeing the clamps she is wearing. If they settled their differences, Mama and Catrina will expect her in the kitchen, helping out. I'm sure the clamps are wreaking havoc on her self-control by now. It will make her count out the minutes until I can put her out of her misery.

LINNET

Dreading facing Mama, I climb up the steps to the front door. My call earlier went unanswered.

I don't know how to tell her that I divorced one son and ended up married to the other son. Dating Bryan is one thing, but a quick marriage like this? Even the most tolerant and affectionate of mothers-in-law would be incredulous.

Some people will think I did it for the money; after all, Bryan is more loaded than his brother.

I thought I'd get eased into Bryan's life slowly, with time to prepare myself and other people, like his mother. But it's just like Bryan to rush into this without consulting me first.

I'm still mad at him, and I hope he will listen to me, because after my talk with his mother, I'm moving out.

I haven't worked out the details, but there's no way I'll stay with a man who doesn't respect me enough to seek and appreciate my opinion on important things like marriage.

He may control my orgasms, but he sure as hell doesn't get to control my life outside the bedroom. I've worked hard on being independent, and this is just ridiculous.

They say that I always run away when things get too hot. This time, I won't run. I'll sit down and have a mature conversation with him. Explain to him my reason for moving out. I know he loves me. But I need to find myself before I get lost in him.

Taking a deep breath, I square my shoulders and press the buzzer. I know I should just push the door and go in, but I feel that I no longer have that right.

Mama opens the door, and I'm surprised—I expected Catrina to do so.

My surprise might have shown.

"Sorry to disappoint you," Mama tells me as she leaves the door open and heads back into the study.

I'm forced to follow her, and my anxiety level shoots to a new high.

Once inside, she locks the door and asks me if I want a drink.

In all the time that I've known Mama, she has only offered me hot chocolate or coffee. I don't know how to take it that she finds it convenient to provide me with something that looks like whiskey. I tried tasting it once, and the mere memory makes my stomach burn.

I take the proffered glass, take a small sip and put it down on the table, then try to sit with the clamps. I hope my discomfort is discreet. It would be terribly embarrassing to have her figure out what's going on. But surely she won't think of something that outrageous. Surely.

"Are you running a fever?" she asks me.

"No, I'm fine."

"Well, you look flushed; if not a fever, then what? I know Bryan's kinky, like his father. Please tell me you don't have any clamps on you."

I cough up the little sip of whiskey and almost spray it. Of all the things I expected from his mother, that caught me unprepared. What kind of family is this?

My shock makes her laugh heartily. I expected to be banned from all the family affairs, but she's taking this as calmly as spotting a little red wine on a white shirt.

"Pardon me, Mama, but I hope I heard you wrong," I gasp, catching my breath.

"A good mother always knows what her kids are up to. Ever since Bryan got into the club life, I've had this worry that he wouldn't settle down and make me a grandmother. But with you in the picture, I suspect I can finally set my worries at ease."

She then proceeds to ask how I got into the club scene.

I wasn't expecting this, either, but there's no point in dissembling, so I just tell her everything.

She seems so innocent; I expected to be condemned. But she's more curious about our club and the safety measures put in place to ensure it is a safe environment for women and men who choose to entrust a total stranger with their bodies.

Once she is satisfied with my answers, she tells me to go into Bryan's room and relax.

I could kiss her right now—not romantically. The clamp has pushed my lips apart, and the friction is making me sweat.

Once in Bryan's room, I change out of my form-fitting dress, and then I notice the glittering ring. I suddenly remember that I didn't tell Mama about the civil wedding I was taken to. She doesn't know just how far my relationship with Bryan has gone, and I would like her to remain ignorant.

It's a lot to deal with, and I set the ring aside. Anyway, I'm still damn sore. I run a bath that I know will do wonders for my abused lady parts.

If I am planning on leaving, on taking care of myself, then I don't think I need to keep these clamps on. But something tells me not to take them off.

With the money I got from Merinda, I can pay for the remaining two seminars required to get my nursing degree.

But now that it's within my grasp, I'm not eager for it. I've spent so much time at the hospital that the thought of working there paralyzes me. All I can think of is Chayla's tiny body in those glass incubators, all the tubes nesting around her tiny body…it's too much. I'd rather stick to office admin.

I wish I had my laptop with me—then maybe I could do something worthwhile while I wait for Bryan. This is the right step to take, stepping back from this rollercoaster life. I could take time to reflect on my life now that I don't have these burdens to carry on my shoulders. Maybe go on a few dates?

I find myself laughing aloud when I think of going out on a date with a guy who isn't Bryan. He's changed everything for me, and the way he makes me feel might be irreplaceable. Now I'll use him as a yardstick to measure other men with, and I'm sure no man will ever measure up.

I know everyone expects me to fold and let Bryan take control of my life. But old habits die hard; I've had to rely on myself ever since my mother passed away. At my age, I can't let a man in and just give him everything. Trust is earned, and it's too early to think that Bryan has attained mine.

Yes, he's taken care of my daughter's treatment, but for a marriage to work, we will need more than gratitude.

God, I'm working myself up.

Once I've toweled off, I sit at the balcony and watch Mama's garden. It always amazed me how the flowers survive Austin's heat, especially at this time of year. Mama once told me that she always plants flowers that are resilient; that way, she doesn't get frustrated with them if they don't make it.

I take my phone and dial Bryan's number. The sooner I get this madness over with, the better it will be.

But from the room I just left, his phone rings.

Curious, I go in to check the source. It wasn't there when I went for my bath. When I came back, I was so wrapped in my issues that I didn't notice anything. I can't find him anywhere in his room, but now that I know he's here, I am anxious. I would hate to be a disappointment to him, but I have to do this for my own sanity.

I decide to put on one of his shirts—I can't put on the dress I had on earlier. With its tightness, it reminds me of the vows I took. Vows that I don't have any intention of keeping.

God, he'll hate me for this. But he should have consulted me first; then I could have told him to wait until I was ready.

"Looking good in my shirt. Tell you what. From now on, you'll only wear my shirts," Bryan tells me as he enters the room from a side door near a dresser.

"You startled me," I point out the obvious, clutching my chest as I try to calm my nerves.

"What are you doing here? You said you would pick me up at five o'clock. It's barely three."

"Sorry to disrupt your relaxation, but I didn't come for you. I brought my daughter to meet and spend some time with her grandmother. They all miss each other too much, and since you'll be otherwise occupied, I thought it would ease your mind knowing Chayla is her with Mama and Catrina. Her nurse is probably going to have a heart attack over her diet, mind you."

"Why?"

"The type of food that those women will be giving Chayla will be very different from what her nurse wants her eating. But don't worry, Mama is a former nurse, as you know, and I had a nutritionist send over all the essential nutrients that we're aiming to have in Chayla's diet."

"Then Chayla will be in heaven. That girl loves good food. It's one thing that I promised her while she was ill." I clear my throat, suddenly feeling a lump in it. My eyes mist over. "I never thought that a day like today was possible—a day where my girl isn't crying out in pain while I watch helplessly.

"There isn't a day that I don't thank the higher powers for this miracle. Thanks, Bryan, for making this possible. I know eventually we would have gotten here, but you shortened the journey. I will forever be grateful for this," I tell him as I get comfortable on the bed. "But Bryan, we need to talk. Please just hear me out first. You guys are accusing me of being a runner. I want to do things the right this time, and…"

"Just hold that thought for a second while I answer this call," he tells me as he leaves the room and goes back to wherever he was earlier.

I wonder if I should follow him; I get the feeling that he didn't want me to finish my train of thought.

But whatever happens, he'll have to listen to me. They won't accuse me of running away again.

chapter TWENTY THREE

BRYAN

I know what Linnet wants to tell me, and I don't care. She wants to put the brakes on our relationship. Whatever she expects to accomplish, it won't happen—not today, not ever. I married her today, and at the end of however long it takes her to come to terms with our relationship, we shall be mated.

Her fate was set in stone the moment I had her name inked on my back. Hell, it was set in stone the moment I saw her.

So I call Rio, who got first dibs on her training, and tell him what I think is happening with Lynn. Rio and Arthur have decided to take on her training, which I know will include her punishment for running away.

Then, once I'm done with the calls, I let her finish her spiel. Just as I guessed, she speaks of not being ready and how she thinks I am taking over her life.

Listening to everything she has to say, I have to admit I'm impressed. The Lynn I met a while ago would have bailed by now. But the fact that she has faced me and told me what she plans on doing is a step in the right direction.

"Lynn, I am happy for what you have decided to do. I am very proud of the woman you are turning out to be. Though you have one misconception—that this is a democracy. That's where you are wrong. Dead wrong."

I remove my shirt and watch her eyes widen a little. She loves my tattoos too much. I know I'm weakening her, and I know she loves it. I never knew my girl had such a thing for bad boys. I'll add a little tattoo on my bicep just for her. I know she'll love it.

I lift her chin so that her beautiful brown eyes are on me. I love this woman, and if she thinks I'll let her go, then she's in for a rude awakening.

"Have you seen my back?"

"Not yet."

"Take your time and have a look at my back and tell me exactly what you were saying before I went to take my call." I try to rein in my temper.

I never lose it, but with her and her continuous refusal to see what we have, I am running out of patience.

I haven't checked my new tattoo, and I promised myself that the first person to look at it would be my mate. When I had it done, I told Caleb to make it as elaborate as possible. And he assured me that once my mate saw it, she would know what she means to me.

She is my everything.

When I hear her gasping, I turn.

"How is it? I haven't checked it out; I wanted you to be the first person to see it."

"It's beautiful. Did you ask him to add all that text on there?"

"What does it say?"

"Below my name, it says, 'You are my everything, and I'll spend the rest of my life proving it,'" she tells me, tracing the delicate script.

"I told him to tattoo something that would show you how much I love you and how I plan to spend the rest of my life making sure that you're happy."

She cries, and I turn to comfort her. I hold her tightly and ease her onto the bed.

I love that she has made herself comfortable in my room. It means she has subconsciously accepted me as her mate. All I have to do now is let her conscious mind catch up with the subconscious one.

I remove the clamps from her labia, loving how red her pussy is. I long to spend the rest of the day here with her showing her how much I love her.

But I will have her after she's sure that she wants me. I might be a bastard, but she's my life, and I'll wait until she says she's ready for me.

So as I ease her pussy lips apart and watch her grow wet, I tell her that for once, I'm in no hurry. Once she is sure, then and only then will I claim my wife and mate.

I can see how frustrated she is, but I know how to cool her off.

So I tell her to put on my briefs together with my shirt. Once she's done, I can tell she thinks we will be staying here, and I know she is plotting to get me to make love to her without her begging, like I promised her.

I love that my girl knows she has me wrapped around her little finger; I don't mind at all.

Then I drop a bomb that I know will cool her off. It's my way of giving Rio the finger. Childish of me, but he made her bolt in the first place. "Looking cute in my clothes. Go downstairs and go through the back door. I'll keep Mama and Chay busy for now. Rio is waiting for you in the kitchen."

When she doesn't make a move towards the door, I warn her not to keep Rio waiting.

"I wouldn't mind having you while your ass is all red and sore, but I want to be the one to make that ass red."

Once she leaves the room, I give Rio the heads up so he can meet her on her way downstairs. I don't want her to get any ideas of getting lost, delaying the inevitable.

chapter TWENTY FOUR

LINNET

I know I decided on moving out of Bryan's life, but damn it—those tattoos showed how much I mean to him. After the ceremony is behind us, I'll make him sit down and discuss his high-handed ways.

By the time I get downstairs, I find Master Rio waiting for me. I can't have him knowing how scared I am to be with him, so I take deep breaths, and by the time I reach him, I'm sure I am calm.

He just gives me his hand and doesn't say anything. Once I am belted into his car, he takes off.

I hold on for dear life; he drives the car like a madman. I am sure we are going to crash, but he handles the car with expertise, and soon, I let my guard down. The ride is exhilarating, and I can't help the giggles that bubble out.

He slows down when we are about to reach the club's gates and avoids crashing through them.

"How bad was it?" he asks with a cocky grin.

Remembering his rules, I tell him the truth—that initially, I thought we were going to crash, but I enjoyed the last part.

"So once you realized I wasn't going to slow down, you decided to enjoy the ride?"

"Yes."

"That's the way it is with your mate; just learn to let go, and I promise you'll enjoy the ride," he tells me as he parks the car.

We enter the club through a side door, and I expect to go straight to the higher level of the club. But he takes me to the main club, and soon, I find myself at the bar.

He doesn't ask me what I'll have, just asks Master H for a Corona and a screwdriver for me.

Drinking dims my senses, and tonight, I want to have all my senses with me.

Then we proceed to the couches, and he points at a place between his knees. He lets me sit down on the mat, then tells me that unless otherwise directed, I am to kneel between his legs.

I feel humiliated and wish that I could throw my drink at him.

"Why did you run?" he asks me calmly.

Always aware of the rule against lying, I explain why I ran.

"Are you planning on running again tonight?"

"No."

"Why?"

"I don't want to put anybody's life at risk."

"I don't see the ladies assisting tonight; they learned their lesson last time."

"I won't run," I promise him.

"Why?"

"I don't want to meet your infamous whip," I tell him honestly.

"What makes you think this life isn't for you? Don't you love Bryan enough?"

I close my eyes and take a deep breath. Panic fills me. How do I even answer that? "Please, sir, I'm not ready to talk about this."

"Then this will take a long time, because until you are ready to talk about it, then and only then shall we proceed. I took a two-month leave from the office so that we can go to one of my places, probably on the beach.

"Once you are ready to open up and talk about what is holding you back, then we can return here and complete the ceremony," he tells me in a conversational tone.

He then scans the club; tonight, the place is full to the brim. I know he longs to be out there with a willing sub.

I take a sip of my screwdriver. It's too sweet. I'd prefer a beer.

The guy has the patience of a saint. We've been here for the last hour, and apart from asking for another Corona and getting me to talk, he hasn't said much.

He is watching me with a hawk's eye, and I feel like a little field mouse under his scrutiny. My knees are starting to complain, and I know I have to do something to get off them.

So I ask him if it's okay to go to the ladies' room.

"Yes, provided you come to look for me. I heard you got lost last time. Don't get lost this time."

Once I'm off my knees, I head straight to the restroom. I'm not pressed, but I needed to give my knees a rest.

I don't take long. I don't want to go looking for him, but on my way back, I'm accosted by a guy I've never laid eyes on.

I try getting rid of him, but he's like a parasite—won't take no for an answer. I swear, if he makes me suffer under Master Rio's whip, I'll hunt him down and slap his dick until he remembers to respect people's answers.

Just then, I see Master Rio heading to the bench room. If he gets there before me, he might decide to tie me up, and I know he'll use his whip.

I then do the only thing I can think of and slap him. My blow strikes his nose but doesn't draw blood. With that, I dart towards Master Rio.

The guy I slap screams like a girl, and I can't help laughing. At least I've taken the edge off my anxiety. I need to hit the gym, though, if running across a crowded bar can wind me like this.

Once I reach Master Rio, I tell him I'm ready to talk, and he takes me upstairs to a red room.

I don't know what the colors indicate, but I've noticed different areas of the building have different color themes.

He takes a seat, and I am left with the bed.

I tell him of my fears, how I would love to have my life in order. I have been relying on myself since I was ten years old, and it's hard just to hand over my control to someone else. I tell him of my dreams and where I want my life to go. I unload all of my fears.

He assures me that I can have it all with Bryan. We talk for a long time before I feel like this really could work if I just focus on having more positive thoughts.

"What you both need in this walk are friends that you can count. Someone who will give you a shoulder to cry on, lend you their strength when you don't have any. And give you endless orgasms, of course.

"Do you know your mate called me the moment he felt you wanted to bail? That's trust, and I feel honored that you've trusted me with your fears, as well. I haven't met my mate yet, but when I do, I'm sure we'll make it because we have the support system we need within the brotherhood.

"I know it's a lot to take on, but what happens is, if you ever have any questions or reservations and feel like you can't talk with Bryan, there's always someone else who you can talk to."

He then explains that it's not wrong to talk to him or any of the brothers that my mate will introduce to me later. But what will be punishable is if I'm going through something that's bothering me and don't make any of them aware of it.

I can't help craving privacy and my own self-reliance. Trusting others? That's still terrifying.

Merinda comes to get me, and I've never been this happy for someone to interrupt such an awkward conversation.

She takes me to a larger room than the one I was in with Master Rio. This room is huge, with mirrors all over the place, even on the ceiling—everywhere I turn, I'm faced with more mirrors.

Sue hugs me, and I can feel the baby kick. "Hello to you, too," I whisper to the baby as I stroke her belly gently.

"Well, don't keep me waiting, or I'll have Junior here kick your ass," she tells me once I hug Jess.

"What am I supposed to tell you other than that I think I'm gonna be sick?" I ask her as I rush to the washroom.

Once I return, Merinda offers me some juice. They are worried about me, but I assure them that whenever I'm stressed, I usually throw up. Right now, my stress levels are extremely high.

"Too bad. I was looking forward to watching you fuck my husband. It's been ages since I last watched the guy in action,"

Jess tells me, as though we're discussing the weather.

I look at the rest of them to gauge their reactions, and no one is surprised—apart from me.

"Okay, why don't you guys tell me what to expect? I won't run. My running days are over, and I think the sooner I get this over with, the better for me."

It's then that Sue tells me that every mated couple is given three brothers to offer support and advice, and if there's any trouble, they solve it.

"If you choose to sleep with any of the brothers, you are allowed to, and you don't need your mate's approval first. The moment he chooses them, he gives them his permission—but I think—I think the brother you call lets your husband know. For us sisters, we always alert each other. For instance, I still call Jessica first before I give Arthur a call. And Merinda here always calls me first. But if you don't want to go through all the hassle, then call an unmated guy. The catch, though, is that each of these guys has their kinks. When you call a guy, you'll have to expect to participate in their kink." She smiles at me, and the normalcy and casualness of it all is starting to penetrate. In some strange way, I like this arrangement.

The rest of me is still shocked. What would people think?

Then again, these are my people now, and they think it's fine. So maybe the only one worried is me, and I don't have to fuss at all…

"Merinda, do you remember the time Master S tied you up?"

"Master Sam loves ropes, but when I called him, I thought he was a safe bet. We were going through some issues with the campaigns and all that. I thought of taking advantage of Sam's beachfront house to relax and think. I was sure Briggs was having an affair with his campaign manager at the time. Sam set me straight, but boy did I enjoy those ropes. Hoping to get a taste of that again before all this is over," she tells me with a straight face.

Is this what my life has turned into?

Somehow, I love it. But I'm still not sure I can handle it.

chapter TWENTY FIVE

Jessica gets a call from Arthur to take me to the boardroom.

"Tell me you didn't rub one out," Sue demands as she rises to her feet. She is so huge, I wonder if she's carrying twins.

"Well, it was a little one, and Bryan made me wear some pussy clamps for so long that I grew numb."

"Well, Arthur loves the contraption in the boardroom, and by the time he's done with you, you'll be singing a new song," Jessica tells me as she leads us down the corridor to what's apparently known as "the boardroom."

Jessica is overly excited, while Sue keeps sending me pitying looks. I want this to be over; then I can talk with Bryan.

My earlier talk with Rio has given me some hope. Maybe there's a way we can make it work.

Once we get into the boardroom, all the members are present, apart from Bryan. I am worried that if he called Rio and told him he thought I wanted to bail, Bryan is still angry at me.

But my worries are uncalled for. I see Bryan come from a doorway that is situated in the farthest corner in an elevated position.

From my view, I don't know what's inside the office, but once I move into the room, I can see it's some sort of contraption.

Arthur looks at me, then comes forward to take my hand. Once we reach where Bryan is standing, he starts undressing me. I keep my eyes on Bryan because I know if I look elsewhere, I'll be overwhelmed, and I might do something I'll later regret.

Once I'm completely naked, Arthur asks me to spread my legs. When I spread them, I can see the desire burning hot in Bryan's eyes, and I know he can see the same in my eyes.

"Briggs, come over here and see how wet she is."

"Will I get a taste?" he asks as he joins Arthur in front of me.

He inserts a finger into my channel, and I buckle, but Arthur holds me firm.

Briggs then kisses my neck, all the way over my shoulders and down my arms, then licks my wetness from his fingers. I'm so primed that I know I'll come within the next few minutes. He kisses his way down my back, and as I try to wrench my gaze from Bryan, he asks me to keep my eyes on him.

Soon, Briggs is bent over my backside, and he inserts another finger through my wetness, while Arthur eats my pussy like he hasn't done it in ages. I can't believe they're doing this with their wives watching.

Can I stand to watch Bryan with another woman?

My mind is brought back to the present when I feel Briggs inserting his finger in my ass. I automatically tense. "Relax, baby, and push against my finger. You'll enjoy it much more," he tells me softly.

Still looking at Bryan, I try to relax, but it's hard with Arthur now finger-fucking me while licking my clit.

I feel when Briggs leaves my side, and I can hear him tear a package. He then tells me to relax as he gives me a gift for being a good girl so far.

He inserts something, and the pain is so unbearable. I try to get away from him, but he is holding me tightly. Once the pain is so sharp, I am sure I'll scream, it pops in, and the sensation is strange. With Arthur's fingers in my pussy and his tongue on my clit, I come with a cry.

Arthur picks me up carefully and places me in the closet-like contraption, and then they open it up completely.

It's roomy inside, but then Rio comes up and removes the walls anyway, saying he wants to get the best view.

Briggs ties my arms to some hooks that are situated above my head, while Arthur ties my legs. The contraption is comfortable, since my weight is evenly distributed.

Then they adjust it so I find myself lying on my back while they lower the top part, which has some brushes hanging down, until it reaches my nipples.

A mirror on the ceiling allows me to see everything they are doing. I can see Arthur with a big dildo and Rio with a bar. Before I can ask what the bar is for, Rio attaches it to my legs, imprisoning me deliciously. It is a spreading bar that will ensure my legs stay apart.

Arthur licks me, and soon, I am wet again. He inserts the dildo and asks me to hold it in—if it falls out at any time, then he'll increase the speed. These people are speaking in tongues, and I can't understand what he's talking about.

Rio then attaches a vibrator to my clit, and I know I can't hold onto Arthur's dildo. They leave me alone and take their seats, like in a real board meeting.

What the fuck! They can't leave me in here like this, tied up with toys everywhere. Bryan comes into my line of vision. He kisses me and tells me anytime I ever need to come alone, without letting him know, to always remember this contraption will be waiting for just such a time.

Once he steps back, the vibrator on my clit starts to buzz while that plug in my ass does the same. I have never felt so full and aroused at the same time, and I come so hard that I cry out. I come and come, and soon, the dildo in my pussy pops out. There's no way I can hold it in.

That's when Arthur comes with a fixed one that's tied to the contraption; once he's done, he increases the speed and I'm coming again, too soon.

I lose track of how many times I come. Soon, I'm begging to be let off. I have learned my lesson. My clit is too sensitive; I can't take it anymore. But the speed doesn't falter, and soon, it hurts. Every orgasm makes me cry out in pain.

I lose track of everything, and next thing I know, I'm in the room we had left earlier, with Jessica and Sue arguing about how many times I came.

"God, guys, remind me to dismantle that thing once I can stand on my legs," I say weakly—at which they all laugh.

Jess tells me it's a good experience when done for pleasure, not for punishment.

"How's your clit? Can I check?"

I look at Jessica as though she's lost her mind.

"Come on, Lynn. I just watched you come a thousand times. I just want a closer look."

I look at Merinda, who seems like the saner one in here, and her face says, *go ahead. It's an adventure you might love.*

"Come on, Jess, what do you want to see? How dark my pussy lips are? Give it a rest. I feel tired, and my nipples have seen better days."

The door then opens, and Arthur walks in. I don't know what he's up to, but by the mischievous look, I know it's no good.

I tense, waiting for whatever he will dish up to me, but he surprises me by going straight for Sue. He kisses her as though she's a long-lost lover. Soon, they're tearing each other's clothes away while the rest of us watch.

I never knew I was such a voyeur, but their making out is turning me on—which is a little bit uncomfortable, since my clit is sore.

Soon, Jess is between my legs, playing with my clit as she watches her husband making out with Sue.

Looking at Merinda, I can see the desire and indecision on her face, and I wonder what has her worried like that.

Rio comes in and starts kissing me, and I kiss him back. For such a cold bastard, he can kiss. Between him and Jessica, I'm lost in the sensations.

Then I feel someone else licking me, together with Jess, and I'm dying to know who else is down there.

When I try to push Rio away so that I can look, Merinda takes one of my nipples in her mouth and sucks hard.

This is an orgy, pure and hot. Soon, Rio stops kissing me and tells me to open up. He is wider than Bryan but a bit shorter. I open for him, and he starts fucking my mouth earnestly.

That's when I realize Merinda has let go of my breasts. I watch as she takes a hard thrust. I'm curious to see who's fucking her this hard. Turning my head—which Rio allows me to do—I come face-to-face with Bryan riding Merinda, answering my earlier question.

I can't believe he's fucking her in front of me, and I want to ask why—but with my mouth stuffed, I think it's hypocritical of me.

Just then, someone starts fucking me, and I push Rio out of my mouth. I have to see who it is—and to my surprise, Briggs is between my legs, thrusting hard.

I check back and watch Bryan fucking Merinda, and without conscious thought, I come so hard that if I didn't have somebody holding me, I would have found myself on the floor.

I am then lifted up as Rio holds me. He opens me up by holding my legs apart, and I watch Arthur getting between my legs. In one thrust, he's inside me. He starts playing with my clit, and I can feel someone playing with my asshole, too.

I have never been claimed there. Nina told me how painful it is, and I never thought I would be tag-teamed like this. I can feel Bryan's eyes on me, and I would give anything to know what he's thinking right now.

After the initial pain is over, Arthur and Rio fuck me together, and I come so hard that I lose it. When I wake up again, I'm in a sterile room with the girls.

Once I open my eyes, Jess is the first to ask me why I lied to them earlier.

"Lied about what?" I ask her.

"You told us that when you're stressed, you usually throw up. But that's not the case, is it, Lynn?" she asks me in a voice that doesn't brook any argument.

Once they've ascertained that I was telling them the truth, they then tell me that I've lost consciousness twice today, so they called for a doctor.

I'm pregnant.

I ask them how Bryan reacted to that, and they tell me they

haven't told him anything yet.

We chat for a bit as I eat some fruit, and then I tell them how I left things earlier in the day.

"Lynn, the sooner you accept that Bryan will always do what he thinks is right for you, and stop fighting him, the better it will be for you and your family. Let me ask—if he didn't marry you today, did you have any intention of marrying him down the road at some time? If the answer is yes, just let it go and start building your future together," Merinda advises.

Once I'm confident that I can get to where Bryan is, I set out to go to him.

I find him with Ben, who excuses himself once I reach them.

I take a seat across from Bryan. When I look at him, all I can see is him pounding away at Merinda.

I'm not jealous, but I wish I knew what to expect and how often it might happen. I know it's hypocritical of me, but it's the way I feel.

He pats his lap, and I know if I sit there, all my worries will melt, forgotten. I shake my head. I can see by the way he's holding himself—I am treading on a thin line.

So I rise, but instead of sitting on his lap, I kneel between his legs. He holds my chin and looks into my eyes; in his eyes, I can see all the questions that he's not going to verbalize.

I have to play my part in this and trust that he loves me enough to listen without thinking of disciplining me. If he does that, I will leave, and damn the consequences. I want to start this life on an equal footing, where I feel my opinion is valued. I am not a second-class citizen or a slave.

So I tell him how I feel now, and how I felt when he took me to sign a marriage certificate without any prior discussions.

He asks me how I felt about the ceremony, and I tell him I wasn't prepared to see him with someone else. It was a shock that I don't how to deal with.

"How about you? How do you feel, knowing you have your reverse harem?"

"I don't know. Before today, I had been with two men, and right now, I don't know how many fucked me. My mind can't go there yet. I need time to process."

"Can you do that while we're together? I need you right now."

He's letting me see how vulnerable he is, and I know I can never deny him anything. He picks me up and holds me tight, and we stay like that for a long time. Then I tell him what Jessica had told me.

"And apart from fatigue, what did the doctor say was your issue?"

I hold his hand, bring it to my stomach and look at him. Before I can say anything, he's kissing me, laughing so loud that I know we'll have an audience soon.

"You've made me the happiest man alive. Please forgive me and let me take you on a honeymoon," he asks me, kissing my stomach.

"Yes, let's go. For once, at least you'll be doing things in their proper manner."

"Which is?"

"Taking me on a honeymoon after the wedding. What else?" I ask.

He carries me out, and from Jessica's laughter, I know she was eavesdropping on us. But I'm so happy, I don't even mind.

EPILOGUE

How did I end up here?

All the disappointments led me to this place. The past is a distance memory that looks more and more like a dream.

I have everything I ever wanted and more—Bryan, Chayla, and soon our little angel who will be joining us in a month's time.

We haven't taken any test to know my child's gender, and Bryan has prohibited Nina from foretelling her fairytales, as he calls them. He knows my friend has incredible intuition, but we don't want to know yet.

When I told Bryan that she knew that Chayla would be a girl before even my first trimester, he forbade her from telling me what she thinks.

Today is a special day—the anniversary of the day I met Bryan at the club and he changed my life. He has a surprise planned, and he won't let me out of the house.

You would think it is my first pregnancy, by the way he takes care of me.

I knew he was up to something when he took Chayla to her grandmother's place.

Now, sitting in our peaceful yard, I am lost in thoughts of our life and how blessed I am when I feel him embrace me from behind.

He then turns me so that I am facing him, I lean towards him, and our lips fall in perfect rhythm, each sweep reminding me of how much I love this amazing man I call my husband.

"You are mine, Linnet," he whispers against my mouth just before he kisses me, his hands inching up my thighs.

I moan in agreement, resting my forehead on him. Tenderly, Bryan looks at me and kisses my eyes and then burrows his head in my shoulder.

"Thank you, sweetheart, for making me complete," he tells me softly.

Our breathing is in sync, rising and falling together and giving us a beautiful song to listen to.

THE END

AMAZON REVIEW

What Did You Think of "My Brother's Wife"?

Thank you for purchasing this book! If you enjoyed reading "My Brother's Wife", I'd love to hear your feedback and hope that you could leave a review on Amazon. Your feedback is very crucial for a newly self-published author like myself and will help me improve future projects. I look forward to reading your reviews!

Please click on the link below, which will take you directly to the book's review page.

Amazon book review link: http://www.amazon.com/review/create-review?&asin=B0833HCJSD

Printed in the USA
CPSIA information can be obtained
at www.ICGtesting.com
LVHW041555090124
768552LV00009B/315